# MR HENRY MULLIGAN

Books by Vernon Coleman include:

The Medicine Men (1975)
Paper Doctors (1976)
Stress Control (1978)
The Home Pharmacy (1980)
Aspirin or Ambulance (1980)
Face Values (1981)
The Good Medicine Guide (1982)
Bodypower (1983)
Thomas Winsden's Cricketing Almanack (1983)
Diary of a Cricket Lover (1984)
Bodysense (1984)
Life Without Tranquillisers (1985)
The Story Of Medicine (1985, 1998)
Mindpower (1986)
Addicts and Addictions (1986)
Dr Vernon Coleman's Guide To Alternative Medicine (1988)
Stress Management Techniques (1988)
Know Yourself (1988)
The Health Scandal (1988)
The 20 Minute Health Check (1989)
Sex For Everyone (1989)
Mind Over Body (1989)
Eat Green Lose Weight (1990)
How To Overcome Toxic Stress (1990)
Why Animal Experiments Must Stop (1991)
The Drugs Myth (1992)
Complete Guide To Sex (1993)
How to Conquer Backache (1993)
How to Conquer Pain (1993)
Betrayal of Trust (1994)
Know Your Drugs (1994, 1997)
Food for Thought (1994, revised edition 2000)
The Traditional Home Doctor (1994)
People Watching (1995)
Relief from IBS (1995)
The Parent's Handbook (1995)
Men in Dresses (1996)

Power over Cancer (1996)
Crossdressing (1996)
How to Conquer Arthritis (1996)
High Blood Pressure (1996)
How To Stop Your Doctor Killing You (1996, revised edition 2003)
Fighting For Animals (1996)
Alice and Other Friends (1996)
Spiritpower (1997)
How To Publish Your Own Book (1999)
How To Relax and Overcome Stress (1999)
Animal Rights – Human Wrongs (1999)
Superbody (1999)
Complete Guide to Life (2000)
Strange But True (2000)
Daily Inspirations (2000)
Stomach Problems: Relief At Last (2001)
How To Overcome Guilt (2001)
How To Live Longer (2001)
Sex (2001)
We Love Cats (2002)
England Our England (2002)
Rogue Nation (2003)
People Push Bottles Up Peaceniks (2003)
The Cats' Own Annual (2003)
Confronting The Global Bully (2004)
Saving England (2004)
Why Everything Is Going To Get Worse Before It Gets Better (2004)
The Secret Lives of Cats (2004)
The Cat Basket (2005)
The Truth They Won't Tell You (And Don't Want You To Know) About The EU (2005)
Living in a Fascist Country (2006)
How To Protect and Preserve Your Freedom, Identity and Privacy (2006)
The Cataholic's Handbook (2006)
Animal Experiments: Simple Truths (2006)
Coleman's Laws (2006)

**novels**
The Village Cricket Tour (1990)
The Bilbury Chronicles (1992)
Bilbury Grange (1993)
Mrs Caldicot's Cabbage War (1993)
Bilbury Revels (1994)
Deadline (1994)
The Man Who Inherited a Golf Course (1995)
Bilbury Pie (1995)
Bilbury Country (1996)
Second Innings (1999)
Around the Wicket (2000)
It's Never Too Late (2001)
Paris In My Springtime (2002)
Mrs Caldicot's Knickerbocker Glory (2003)
Too Many Clubs And Not Enough Balls (2005)
Tunnel (1980, 2005)

**as Edward Vernon**
Practice Makes Perfect (1977)
Practise What You Preach (1978)
Getting Into Practice (1979)
Aphrodisiacs – An Owner's Manual (1983)

**with Alice**
Alice's Diary (1989)
Alice's Adventures (1992)

**with Donna Antoinette Coleman**
How To Conquer Health Problems Between Ages 50 and 120 (2003)
Health Secrets Doctors Share With Their Families (2005)

# MR HENRY MULLIGAN

Vernon Coleman

Chilton Designs

Published by Chilton Designs, Publishing House, Trinity Place,
Barnstaple, Devon EX32 9HG, England.

First published by Chilton Designs in 2007

ISBN: 1 898146 01 2

A catalogue record for this book is available from
the British Library.

Printed by Antony Rowe Limited, Wiltshire

# DEDICATION

To Donna Antoinette with all my love. A human island of generosity, loyalty and integrity in a world which too often seems overrun by the wicked, the cruel and the thoughtless. An island offering respite in a turbulent ocean.

# PROLOGUE

H enry had been in hospital for a long time.
We'd first met in the teaching hospital in Birmingham, during my finals examination in 1971. He'd only been in hospital a day or so then and he had been one of my 'short cases'. I don't know how they do it these days but the routine for examining final year medical students was simple and straightforward but nerve-wracking. A visiting examiner, usually a senior consultant from another medical school, took a student to see three patients. Usually these were patients who had been brought into the hospital specially for the day. Sometimes they would be patients who had been recently admitted to the hospital but who had not yet been seen by students.

My 'long case' had gone reasonably well and I'd successfully diagnosed the first two of my 'short cases'. The examiners had been relatively human. Now I just had one more hurdle to overcome. If I acquitted myself reasonably well I would probably pass and mutate, overnight, from medical student to doctor. From reckless and irresponsible to a responsible, respected member of the community in just a few hours.

'Henry is 72-years-old,' said the examiner, standing at the end of the bed and rather airily waving a hand in Henry's direction. At the bottom of the bed, where a clipboard containing the patient's temperature chart is usually hooked over the bottom rail, there was nothing. The clipboard had gone; safely stored in an office somewhere. In its place there was a piece of paper Sellotaped to the bed frame. 'Henry Mulligan. Aged 72.' That was all I was getting.

The examiner was Scottish and spoke with a broad accent which I could barely understand. When he waved his arm about, two inches of starched cuff slipped back a little and what looked like, and probably was, a gold Rolex flashed in the sunlight. 'Without getting closer than the end of the bed I want you to tell me what's wrong with him.'

I smiled at Henry. I felt embarrassed, partly because of the doctor's rudeness and partly because of what I was doing. Although I was close to being a doctor I was conscious that I was still a medical student, still not yet thoroughly accustomed to staring at total strangers. I loathed and despised consultants who treated patients with no more respect than they treated histology specimens in the laboratory.

'The thumb is missing from his left hand,' I said quickly.

'Bravo,' said the examiner. 'Does it appear to be a recent loss?'

'No, sir.'

'Quite right,' said the examiner. 'Mr Mulligan lost his thumb when he was sixteen. An industrial accident. It has no relevance to his current stay in hospital and nor, indeed, to your future.'

I studied Mr Mulligan again. 'He's not yellow is he?' I asked. There aren't many diagnoses which can be made from simply looking at a patient from a distance. Especially when all you have to look at is a face and two hands. Jaundice was an easy and obvious possibility.

The consultant stared at Henry and then at me. 'No, he's not,' he said. 'But you get no marks for spotting things that he isn't.' He sounded bored. 'If you're going to give me a list of things he's not then we're going to be here a very long time. To save us both time, he's not pregnant, he hasn't got measles and he's not dead either.' He smiled and displayed two rows of perfectly capped and polished teeth. He looked like a shark. 'I'm not always this helpful,' he said. 'You must be charming me.'

Now I knew. The consultant was one of the sarcastic ones. I felt the sweat breaking out on my brow and wondered whether it would be better to leave it there or to wipe it away. I stared at Henry again. All I could see of him was still just his face, neck and hands. It really wasn't a lot on which to form a diagnosis. Six years learning seemed to have disappeared as quickly as water down a drain.

'Does he have any symptoms?' I asked the consultant.

'He may do. Indeed, I would go so far as to say that it is extremely likely. Despite the generosity of the health service I doubt if he would be taking up a bed if he had no symptoms. This is not my hospital but I doubt if your superiors will have stocked their beds with healthy passers-by taken from the streets. Your task here is to make a diagnosis simply by standing where you are and using your eyes and whatever cerebral tissue the good Lord chose to give you.'

I stared again. Henry's hands and wrists seemed normal. No signs of arthritis. No Dupuytren's contracture. No clubbing. No skin lesions. His hair was thinning but baldness would hardly be the diagnosis the inquisitor was looking for. Both eyes seemed normal. Pupils the same size. Or were they? Was one a little smaller than the other? He had dark brown eyes and from this distance it wasn't easy to be sure. One eyelid seemed to be drooping a little. Did he have a seventh facial nerve paralysis. Henry, staring back at me, allowed a twitch of a smile. The corners of both sides of his mouth moved together. No seventh nerve paralysis. No Bell's Palsy.

'His breathing seems a little laboured,' I said, rather desperately.

'So is yours,' sneered the consultant immediately. 'But it's hardly a diagnosis, is it?' He looked at his watch, lifted it closer to his ear and shook it as though wondering if it had stopped. Some consultants develop these little bits of play-acting. They think they're being funny.

I stared at the patient again. There was some redness on the man's cheeks. It wasn't a lot. Hardly there really. And I was certain there was some drooping to one eyelid. The right one.

Just then the ward sister approached. She was carrying a small piece of folded paper.

'I'm sorry to bother you, sir,' I heard her whisper. She oozed deference and ingratiation. 'There's a telephone message for you.'

I was still staring at Henry. He lifted a finger and touched his cheek. Then he touched his right eyelid. The movement looked perfectly natural. But I knew it wasn't. Some patients have been known to give students a clue. Maybe these were clues. On the other hand some patients have been known to deliberately mislead students.

The examiner had opened the note and was reading it.

I was sure now that Henry's cheeks were slightly red. And there was a slight droop to one eyelid. If only I could see the pupil a little better. I glanced at the ward clock. I had less than two minutes to make a stab at a diagnosis. But what the hell was it? Patients with a type of heart disease known as mitral stenosis will sometimes have very red cheeks. It's not common. I'd never seen it. But if teaching hospitals specialise in anything it is the rare and unusual.

A drooping eyelid can be a sign of many things but it can be part of something called Horner's Syndrome: a possible sign of lung cancer.

The trouble was that I now had two quite separate diagnoses. One diagnosis would be good. Two was twice as many as I needed. But Mr Mulligan had definitely touched both his cheek and his eyelid. If he had been giving me a hint he had been giving me two hints. Two clues.

The examiner folded the note and slipped it into his jacket pocket. 'Thank you sister,' he murmured. The sister paused for a moment, as though wondering whether or not she should curtsey, and then backed away down the ward. 'Are we any closer to a diagnosis?' he asked me.

I thought hard. My brain was racing and sweat was dripping into my eyes. Underneath my white coat my shirt was soaked and clinging to my back. I had two possible diagnoses. But which one should I choose? I had been taught that I should always try to fit a patient's signs and symptoms into a single diagnosis. But I knew of nothing that could cause reddened cheeks and a droopy eyelid.

'I suspect that Mr Mulligan has two problems,' I said softly, taking my future by the throat. I had turned away from the patient's bed. I felt uncomfortable about announcing my diagnosis in front of him, though I knew that he would already have been told what was wrong with him and warned to ignore the diagnostic ravings of medical students. 'He has mitral stenosis and pulmonary carcinoma.'

'You suspect?' said the examiner. He glowered at me. 'The verb 'suspect' is a very uncertain word. I don't like uncertain doctors.'

'Mr Mulligan has mitral stenosis and pulmonary carcinoma,' I whispered.

'Two diagnoses?' said the examiner. 'You have one patient but you're giving me two diagnoses?'

I nodded. I would have to spend another year at medical school and then resit my finals in twelve months' time. I had heard of students who had failed their finals three times.

'Do you have a Guardian Angel whispering in your ear?'

'No, sir.'

'Do you believe in miracles?'

'Possibly, sir.'

'Well I certainly do now,' said the examiner. Another little joke. 'You're absolutely right. Mr Mulligan has mitral facies caused by mitral stenosis and he has developed Horner's syndrome as a result of developing pulmonary cancer.'

'Thank you, sir,' I murmured.

'Nothing whatsoever to thank me for, doctor,' said the examiner. 'Congratulations.'

Before his words had properly sunk in he had turned and was walking away, heading for the sister's office and the telephone. Abandoned, I stood at the end of Henry's bed. Two words had changed my future. Doctor. Congratulations. It was over. I had qualified.

Still in a daze, I thanked Mr Mulligan and shook his hand. He smiled and congratulated me. I was still too traumatised to take it in. I left the ward, went to the hospital canteen and celebrated with a cup of weak coffee and a stale doughnut.

# CHAPTER 1

Twelve months later I was finishing my pre-registration year's work as a junior hospital doctor and Henry was still a patient in the hospital where I had first met him. I was working on the male geriatric ward as the resident junior doctor (the doctor on the very bottom rung of the hospital hierarchical ladder, the one who gets up in the middle of the night, appears on Sunday afternoon when a new patient has to be admitted and turns up at odd hours of the day and night to take blood samples, deal with day-to-day emergencies and, in view of my height, fit fresh light bulbs into the fitting in the ward sister's office). Henry, who had been thrown out of the acute medical ward because they could no longer think of anything positive to do with him, was a patient there. He wasn't well enough to go home. He wouldn't have been well enough to go home without full-time nursing care. Since he lived in a caravan with a wife who was ill, he stayed in hospital.

We were both on Windom ward because it was a place for people who weren't wanted anywhere else. Henry wasn't wanted anywhere else because he was considered incurable; beyond medical redemption. Patients died every day on Windom ward. It was what people seemed to do best there. It was certainly what they were expected to do. Patients were dumped on the ward because there wasn't anything else that could be done for them and they weren't well enough to go home or be deposited in an old people's home.

I was there because I'd annoyed too many important people to get a job on a fashionable ward where exciting things were happening. Over my years as a medical student I had found a number of ways of upsetting the establishment hierarchy. Putting me on Windom ward was, in their eyes, a punishment.

But even though we had ended up in the same place because we weren't wanted anywhere else (or considered good enough to be anywhere else) my future was still considerably brighter than Henry's. I was about to become a fully registered medical practitioner, entitled to escape from the hospital and work as a general practitioner without supervision. Henry had a big T stamped on his medical notes in red ink. He was terminally ill and the consultant responsible for his destiny had decreed that if there was an emergency Henry was not to be resuscitated. No one thought he was worth bothering about. He was old and unimportant. He wasn't, and never had been as far as anyone knew, a man of significance or substance. He was just another dull, old man waiting to die. So, why bother doing anything to delay the inevitable? No one would dare admit it but that was the official policy. Of course, if he'd ever been important, or related to someone important, things would have been different.

During the twelve months we had known one another Henry Mulligan and I had become good friends. I sometimes wondered if I would have qualified without the confidence he had given me. That touch on his cheek and the touch on his eyelid hadn't given me the answers but they had given me clues and, more importantly, the confidence without which I would once again be standing there sweating while an impatient examiner stood behind me shaking his watch. I felt a great debt to him but there was far more to our relationship than that. I had learned more about real life and about people from Henry than I had learned from any doctor or teacher. Often, at night, we would talk in the day room. He didn't sleep well and he would sit there, in his wheelchair, reading quietly: a solitary and lonely figure, lit by the light from a single wall lamp. If I was called to the ward I would pop in to see how he was and I would end up sitting and talking. Or, rather, sitting and listening.

It was difficult for him to talk. His deteriorating heart and his lung cancer meant that every breath was an effort, and every word had to be hewn out of what little strength he had left. It meant that he weighed his words with special care and laid them before me with the caution and precision of a poet.

He told me something about his life. His parents had been poor. His father had worked on the dustcarts and hadn't learned to read until he was 26. He'd taught himself so that he could make sure that his son wouldn't have an illiterate father. His mother had cleaned office floors at night. They had both worked until they'd died. 'Kind, honest, decent people. Salt of the earth,' was how Henry described them. 'Exploited' he added, the bitterness showing through.

Henry's formal education had ended when he'd left school at fourteen. He had worked as an apprentice at a small engineering factory in the West Midlands. Wolverhampton. Willenhall. Wednesbury. Walsall. Somewhere in that area. At nights he'd studied maths and engineering as part of his apprenticeship but, with an unquenchable thirst for knowledge, he'd also studied English (language and literature) and History.

'When I was a teenager I believed that the truth would set us free,' he said, wistfully. 'But the innocent days didn't last long. The more I discovered the more discontented I became. The truth does not make us free but it does make us angry, frustrated and bitter. It makes us conscious of our own impotence and of the extent of the evil which surrounds us.'

★★★

I got into the habit of taking a flask of hot water, two mugs and some Earl Grey tea bags into the hospital with me. Henry loved a cup of tea but hated the stuff the hospital served up. 'It's brown and milky and doesn't taste of anything,' he complained.

We were drinking tea at six o'clock one morning in the day room. The night staff were still on duty and breakfast was still an hour or so away. Henry couldn't sleep, as usual, and I didn't see any point in going back to bed. I had a patient who was seriously ill. I knew I would have to go and see him in half an hour so I sat with Henry for a while.

'My father was in this hospital just before he died,' said Henry.

'In fact he died here, though not on this ward. When my father was dying he said something that, at the time, I thought was very sad,' said Henry. 'He said that there was no-one in the world who called him by his first name. All his friends and work-mates were dead, or too sick to visit him. My mother had gone years before. All his relatives were either dead or out of touch. The only people he saw were the nurses and the doctors, who all called him Mr Mulligan, and me. And I called him Dad.'

Henry sipped at his tea. 'He wanted me to call him by his Christian name. He was Henry too. But I couldn't bring myself to do it. It didn't seem right. I know kids do it these days but back then it seemed like blasphemy.'

'So, what did you do?'

'I had a word with the doctor and got the doctor to call him Henry.'

I smiled at him. 'Did your father enjoy that?'

'Very much,' nodded Henry. 'He didn't know I'd arranged it and he told me about it with great glee.'

'That's a nice story,' I told him.

'But it's only half the story,' said Henry. He sipped again at his tea. He always sipped at his tea, like a man drinking a fine malt whisky. 'Do you know I can't remember when anyone called me Mr Mulligan.'

I looked at him, frowning. I didn't quite understand.

'Everyone I meet calls me Henry,' he said. 'Every doctor, every nurse, every porter, every cleaner, every clerk – they all call me Henry.' He waved a hand. 'I go down to the X-ray department and the girl at the desk calls me Henry. The radiographer calls me Henry. The porter who brings me back calls me Henry. I go down to the lab and the technicians call me Henry. Oh, I know it's not just me. They do it to everyone. They call all the patients by their Christian name. They all call each other by their Christian names too.' He paused and stared at his tea. 'There's no dignity to it. There isn't the joy of reaching that moment in a relationship between two people when formality is dropped and people get on first name terms. That's what it used to be called. Being on first name terms.

It meant that you knew one another well and that you were friends rather than just acquaintances.'

I didn't know what to say. I was as guilty as everyone else and I saw his point. Actually, I didn't just see his point, I knew he was right.

We sat in silence, the weak, morning sunlight filtering in through the day room windows.

'Would you like more tea, Mr Mulligan?' I asked him at last.

He looked at me, saw that I was serious, and held out his cup. 'Thank you doctor,' he said. 'That's very kind of you. I don't mind if I do.'

I filled his cup and then filled mine and put the now empty flask down on the table in front of us. We sat there, sipping at our tea and watching the day break.

★★★

After that I addressed Henry as Mr Mulligan and I addressed Daphne as Mrs Mulligan. Henry, in turn, addressed me as doctor. Daphne could hardly ever remember my name but when she did it was still my Christian name, which I didn't mind a bit.

More importantly, I always referred to Henry as Mr Mulligan when I was talking about him to other members of the hospital staff. And the funny thing is that it stuck with quite a lot of them. Nurses and porters and even other doctors referred to him as Mr Mulligan and called him Mr Mulligan when they spoke to him. And then I did the same thing with other patients too. Instead of referring to them by the Christian names I referred to them by their surnames.

★★★

A week or two later we were sitting in the day room drinking tea. I can't remember what we were talking about.

'Would you like more tea, Mr Mulligan?' I asked him, holding up the flask. 'There's still a cup each left.'

'Do you know,' he said, looking at me. 'I think we know each other well enough to dispense with the formalities. Why don't we address one another by our Christian names?'

'On first name terms?'

'On first name terms.'

I thought about it for a moment. 'On one condition,' I said at last. 'Only when we're alone. When we're with other people – or when we are talking about one another to other people – we stick to surnames. You're still Mr Mulligan.'

Henry didn't even think about it. He held out a hand. I put down the flask and grasped it.

'It's a deal,' he said. 'A gentleman's agreement.'

★★★

'Today we celebrate,' said Henry. He took a miniature whisky bottle out of one dressing gown pocket and two bars of chocolate from the other.

'What are we celebrating?'

'Every day from now on is a bonus,' said Henry. 'It was exactly six months ago that my consultant gave me six months to live.'

'So you should be dead by now?'

'Exactly.'

'You look well for dead.'

'I feel well for dead.'

'Doctors shouldn't make prognoses like that,' I said.

'They shouldn't,' said Henry. 'I hope you never will. Doctors can kill people that way.'

I took a bite from the bar of chocolate he'd given me and waited.

'Since I've been in here,' he said, 'I've known three people who've died because they were told they were dying.'

'You can't know that,' I argued.

He shrugged. 'Pretty certain of it,' he said. 'They were all told by their consultant that they would be dead within a specific time period. Same chap who told me when I'd die. They all fretted about it. They all regarded the date as though it was an execution date.'

'And they died near to it?'

'No. They died on it. Bang on the button.'

I ate more chocolate and felt a shiver down my spine.

'Voodoo,' said Henry. 'Plain, old-fashioned voodoo. If you live in a primitive village and the man in the warpaint and chicken feathers tells you that you're going to die then you die. Here we're a bit more sophisticated. The man handing out the death sentences wears a white coat instead of warpaint and chicken feathers.'

# Chapter 2

Amanda Pettigrew was short and slim. She had short, dark hair, a cute nose and such an improbably large bust that she was known to everyone as Mae. Her bosom stretched her jumpers close to breaking point. Once, when she walked into the Coronary Care Unit to deliver some missing medical notes, she had caused chaos. Five monitors went off all at once as male patients responded to her appearance. Of the remaining four patients two were asleep, one was female and 83-years-old and one had died and was waiting to be wheeled down to the mortuary.

Amanda worked in the medical records office and had a very well-developed affection for the good life. She had no qualifications and regarded learning as something other people did so that they could be of more use to her. She said she didn't see the point in qualifications. 'I can always be a model or read the news on the television,' she said, pointing out that she could walk while wearing clothes and she could read while sitting down, and that knowing how to do anything else would be superfluous. Her work in the medical records office was, I suppose, an essential part of her husband acquisition programme. Even then I wasn't sure why we were together for we had absolutely nothing in common.

Her father was a dentist who also owned a growing chain of estate agents. I was never quite sure whether he was a dentist who dabbled in selling houses or an estate agent who dabbled in bridge work and root canals. Either way he was obsessed with making money. It was his job, his hobby and his passion.

Amanda's mother's obsession was spending money and I suppose that made Mr and Mrs Pettigrew pretty well suited for one another. 'If they ever create an Olympic event for shoppers my wife will be the first pick for the British team,' said Mr Pettigrew, with some pride, adding that as sport became ever-increasingly commercial he didn't regard the prospect of such an event as an impossibility. Mr and Mrs Pettigrew were keen to establish what they called 'a position' in local society and to this end they held regular fund-raising dinners to which they would invite a wide variety of local worthies. They served up expensive food and even more expensive wine and collected donations for their favourite charity of the moment. Someone who had attended one of their seemingly well-intentioned soirées confided that if the Pettigrews had forgotten about the dinners and just written a cheque for a quarter of what they spent on food and wine the charity of the moment would have done twice as well.

Amanda and I had met at one of those curious parties which are held at regular intervals in the junior doctors' mess. Vast quantities of cheap food (usually from a local Chinese take away) and cheap wine (invariably bought by the crate from a local supermarket) were provided free of charge by a drug company keen to indoctrinate young doctors before they went out into the real world of general practice and started prescribing serious quantities of drugs. The party would usually start with a short, ten minute film about one of the organising company's products. The company's representative would then hand out pens, notepads, diaries and other marketing flim flam before taking the tops off all the silver foil dishes from the take-away and declaring the meeting closed and the party started. Since the parties were usually held in the junior doctors' living area there wasn't much chance of keeping out of the way. Anyone could turn up and it wasn't unusual for us to stagger out of our bedrooms the following morning and find a patient or two, sometimes still complete with drip stands, sitting snoring in a corner; pyjamas or nightie stained with sweet and sour and paint-stripping Chianti.

We met about three months before the end of my second six-month stint as a junior house officer. Within a few weeks we had become a couple. I had met her parents (both of whom had shown little interest in anything other than my potential earning power, and my ability to keep their daughter well supplied with a copious quantity of those two essentials of the rising classes, shoes and handbags) and Amanda's conversation had turned, with ominous speed and ease, to the drawbacks of shagpile carpeting and the long-term benefits of double-glazing.

Amanda made it clear that she was planning to give up her job and follow in her mother's footsteps as a full-time housewife. She also made no secret of the fact that she expected to have staff to deal with the day to day trivia of shopping, cleaning, cooking, washing, ironing and so on, leaving her free to deal with the more sophisticated business of choosing costume accessories.

We (or rather she) had decided to celebrate the end of my pre-registration year with a two week holiday on the island of Corfu. I hadn't had a proper holiday for years but Amanda, whose parents supplemented her hospital salary with a generous clothes and holiday allowance, had travelled widely in her search for a perfect suntan and more shoes. She produced a brochure, got me to write a cheque and booked the holiday. I was looking forward to a rest and had already filled a suitcase with paperback books I was looking forward to reading. I had not told Amanda this. We had once had a rather confused conversation as a result of her belief that the words 'book' and 'catalogue' were synonymous.

Four days before we were due to fly off Amanda rang and said she wanted to meet me in the cafeteria to discuss our future. I found this prospect rather alarming but was greatly relieved when she announced that the holiday and the relationship were both 'off'. She had, she told me with no suspicion of regret or embarrassment, also been having a serious relationship with a manager in one of her father's estate agency shops. My long working hours must have made it easy for her to see Roderick and I suppose she probably told Roderick that she was having her nails done when she was seeing me.

'Roderick and I are going to Crete,' she told me. 'We're getting married later in the year. He's got an MGB and a three bedroomed detached house on the new development Dad's handling for the builders. It's not a starter home. It's an executive residence.'

I was greatly relieved at this unexpected change in my circumstances but did my best not to show it. Amanda wouldn't have noticed if I had. She was too busy telling me about the price of the carpets and curtains they'd chosen. She said she'd known about this plan for some weeks but that she'd decided to leave it until I'd finished my second pre-registration house job so that I'd be too busy celebrating to feel downcast at the news. I told her that I appreciated her thoughtfulness and she said she always liked to treat people nicely because you never knew when you might need them. 'Who knows,' she said, 'you might become a plastic surgeon and be able to save my life one day.'

She told me that she had gone out with me to see if she really loved the estate agent but that in the end she'd decided she didn't love the estate agent at all but would marry him because his financial prospects were so much better than mine. 'Even if you go into general practice you won't earn as much as Roderick is earning for at least a decade.' 'Daddy checked out the figures for me,' she said. 'And Roderick gets better holidays too,' she added.

As soon as she'd left I telephoned the travel agent and tried to cancel the trip to Corfu. The girl I spoke to said it was too late to cancel and that I wouldn't get a refund unless I could show exceptional personal circumstances. I told her my girlfriend had left me and was going off with an estate agent. This news seemed to trigger memories with the travel agent. She told me that her boyfriend had left her to go off with a dental hygienist who was (in her words) 'no better than she ought to be' and 'a cheap tart'. She (the travel agent not the dental hygienist) asked if I was depressed. I lied and said that I felt like killing myself. She said she did too but that it passed. She said she couldn't give me a refund, though. She then gave me her home telephone number and told me to ring her if I was able to go to a party with her the following Saturday. I didn't write the number down.

I didn't have another job to go to. I didn't have a girlfriend. I wasn't going on holiday. I had a new certificate entitling me to work as a general practitioner. But that was about all I did have. To be honest, I felt at a bit of a loose end.

And then something happened that made Amanda's decision to dump me definitely fortuitous.

★★★

Junior house jobs last for six months. At the end of the six months the hospital finds another young doctor and the exiting incumbent, by now pale, exhausted and sucked dry by hard working days and sleepless nights, is discarded; used up and shell-shocked. It's a long journey from carefree, irresponsible medical student to being a doctor responsible for scores of lives and hundreds of life or death decisions every week. But it's a journey that takes no time at all. One day I was a medical student; my only real concern the examinations ahead of me. Days later I was a hospital doctor; with no time at all for personal thoughts. Life flashed by as though I was on a motorway.

In those days, the early 1970's, there were no rules governing the hours young doctors were allowed to work. During my two house jobs I don't think I ever worked less than 100 hours a week. And that wasn't counting the interrupted nights I spent on call; collapsing into a coma in between telephone calls and beeps from bright and cheery night nurses. 'Oh, doctor, can you come to Windom Ward please. Mrs Jamieson's drip has come out again.' 'Oh, doctor, can you pop along to Albert Ward and sign a prescription for Mr Jennings. He can't get to sleep and needs a tablet.' On several occasions I actually managed to clock up 168 hours work in a single week. Naturally, there was no overtime and sympathy was in equal short supply.

The night nurses would go off duty in the early morning, handing over to the daytime shift, wrapping themselves up in their blue-lined cloaks and scurrying back to have huge fried breakfasts in the canteen before going back to bed. Some nurses preferred working nights. They slept for five or six hours and spent their afternoons shopping and going to deserted cinemas. But while they slept or shopped the junior doctors just kept on working. "We Never Close" should have been our motto. I saw young doctors fall asleep while leaning against a wall. The calls from the wards came so thick and fast that we got used to eating three course meals in five minutes or less. Spooning in the custard before the soup had finished its journey down the oesophagus. Indigestion? Too young for that. The payment for this lifestyle would be made in later years.

My six months contract as junior house officer for Windom Ward had ended. It was the second of my six month pre-registration hospital jobs. I was now fully qualified.

It was my last day on the ward; my last day in my job; my last day at the hospital where I had spent every working hour since I'd qualified; my last day as a hospital doctor. It was the first day of a new life with no job, no commitments and no home. Everything I owned that I wasn't wearing was in a suitcase and a small bag. Since I'd qualified I'd lived in a hospital room for a year. The room went with the job. Now I didn't have a job I didn't have a room either. I had to find somewhere to stay. I had £12 in cash and £137 in the bank.

I had handed over my ward, my patients and my responsibilities to my successor, a frighteningly fresh and innocent looking young doctor who had been qualified for two days. He looked too young to have started shaving. His cheeks were pink and freshly scrubbed, his eyes were bright and sparkled with excitement. The pockets of his freshly starched white coat were stuffed with instruments and notebooks filled with revision notes. I couldn't help wondering what he'd done wrong to get this job. No newly qualified doctor with ambitions wanted a job on a geriatric ward. It was regarded as a dead-end job; a career backwater suitable only for those who had no future and no medical ambitions. The young guns, those junior doctors hoping for medical fame and fortune, all wanted to work on the heart unit or in paediatric neurology.

I tried to think back to when I had started my first hospital job. Had I ever been so innocent, fresh and full of energy? Of course I had. But I couldn't remember it. I was too damned tired. I was too damned tired to remember what I'd done the day before let alone how I'd felt a year earlier. I caught sight of myself in a mirror in the staff washroom. I seemed to have aged ten years since I'd qualified.

I went back to the ward for one final time to say goodbye to the staff and the patients who had been my life for twenty six weeks. I shook hands and kissed cheeks with people I knew I would never see, speak to or hear from again and we promised to keep in touch with one another. 'People always say this and never do but it'll be different with us, won't it?' said a nurse whose name I had already forgotten. 'Would you have a look at Mr Kendall's drip before you go? The new doctor put it up and it isn't working properly.'

Henry Mulligan wasn't there. His bed was empty. But he hadn't just gone down to have an X-ray. The bed had been stripped. And his locker was bare.

I poked my head round the door to the office. Sister Tomkins, the ward sister, was in there. She looked harassed. She always looked harassed. She was in her early forties and lived with her mother. She was kind and caring and made from the sort of material there's a shortage of these days.

'Where's Mr Mulligan gone?' I asked. For months Henry had been too weak to walk. Even to move about the ward he had to be in a wheelchair. And he was too frail to wheel himself more than a couple of feet.

'Oh, don't ask,' she replied.

'No, where is he?'

'He's been stolen.'

I stared at her.

'He's been stolen,' she repeated. 'I'm having a terrible day. Henry has been stolen and the night staff mislaid a bottle of nitrazepam.'

'Who would steal Henry?' I asked her. 'Why?' As much as I loved him I couldn't see anyone wanting to ransom him. Who would pay? With what?

The sister shrugged. 'I have no idea,' she said. She sounded tired and exasperated. 'You knew him better than anyone,' she said. 'Have you got any ideas?'

'When did anyone last see him?'

'I saw him yesterday at supper time. No one seems to remember seeing him since then. He had his supper in the day room. He was in his wheelchair watching television.'

'Was anyone else in there?'

'No. He was by himself.'

'And no one remembers putting him to bed?'

'No.'

'Where's all the stuff that was in his locker.'

Sister Tomkins nodded to a plastic bag on the floor. 'In there.'

'No one else in the hospital has seen him?'

'Not that I know of.'

'What are you going to do?

'I'll have to put him down as a voluntary discharge.'

'But he couldn't discharge himself,' I pointed out.

'I know,' agreed the sister. 'But what's the alternative? We didn't discharge him and if I report him as stolen everyone will think I've gone barmy.'

'You're not going to tell the police?'

'Tell the police? Tell them what? That I've mislaid a patient? They'd laugh themselves silly. Besides, I don't want the police round here now that some idiot on nights has lost a bottle of nitrazepam. I bet it was that stupid bloody Ecclestone girl. She's away with the fairies most of the time. She's fallen out with her boyfriend and she doesn't know what day it is. She's probably left them in the sluice or posted them to her granny.'

I knew why Henry had gone. And who with. I also knew he'd taken the nitrazepam. I was just relieved that no one else seemed to have connected Henry's disappearance with the disappearance of the sleeping pills. Nurse Ecclestone could take care of herself if the Sister bawled her out. She'd done plenty of things for which she'd never been blamed.

'What are you going to do with his stuff?' I asked.

'Stuff it in a cupboard somewhere in case he comes back, I suppose.'

'Let me have it. I'll take it to his wife.'

'Do you know where she lives?'

'Yes.'

I thought I could find him. I thought I knew him well enough. In fact, though I didn't know it at the time, of course, I hardly knew him at all.

The sister bent down, picked up the plastic bag and handed it to me. 'Take it,' she said. I took the bag from her, opened it and peered inside. There wasn't much. A book. A couple of envelopes. A few items of clothing. Not much to show for a life but I suspected Henry must have left in a hurry to have had to leave them behind.

'It was odd,' said the sister, remembering something.

I looked at her.

'Some of the stuff – the box and the envelopes – was already in the plastic bag by the side of his bed. The rest of the stuff – the clothes – were still in the locker.'

The bag had been packed but had either been forgotten or dropped. I'd take it to him. If I found him in time.

'How's your mother?' I asked her. She had talked about her mother often. She loved her but knew that she had given the best years of her life to look after her. Duty had overwhelmed her sense of self.

'She's a pain in the butt. I'm going to book her on a cruise when I can find one that goes to the Bermuda Triangle.'

'Good idea.'

'Why are you doing this?' asked Sister Tomkins. She nodded towards the plastic bag full of Henry's belongings.

'Because I owe him.'

'You mean because of what happened during your finals?'

'That's a part of it,' I said. 'But it's not just that. He taught me more than I learnt from a hundred professors, lecturers and tutors. Just by being him. He taught me things I didn't know I didn't know because no one had ever told me about them. And he taught me about me. He did it without ever teaching me anything but just by being. I hate to think of the sort of doctor I would have become if I hadn't known him.'

'But those things you learned because you were ready to learn them.'

The truth was that because of Henry I had found myself more able to see the patient's point of view. In any dispute with authority I took sides with the patients and felt increasingly irritated by and ill at ease with the arrogance and pomposity of doctors and nurses.

'You mustn't allow yourself to become emotionally involved with the patients,' said a stern senior registrar late one Saturday night. 'You have to keep your distance and protect yourself from any sort of emotional attachment. You're a professional and must remain aloof, distant and impartial.'

I could neither accept nor even understand this viewpoint. Removing the caring and concentrating on the curing seemed to me then (and, over thirty years later, still does) to be a cheap cop out; an excuse to avoid spoiling the sense of authority which both doctors and nurses then enjoyed (a sense of authority long since requisitioned by administrators) with too great a sense of personal responsibility.

I didn't say anything to the sister, though this was not because I didn't think she would understand (in retrospect, I think she would have) but because I feared that she might consider my attitude a sign of weakness and immaturity.

'And you care about him don't you?'

I smiled at her. 'Of course I do. I care about them both. They're a remarkable couple.'

'You think something will happen to them?'

I nodded.

'You think he'll do something...'

'...silly?' I finished the cliché for her.

'Yes.'

I nodded.

'And you want to stop him?'

'I don't know about that,' I admitted. 'I don't know that I have that right. I don't know that I could or should. But I want to say goodbye.'

Sister Tomkins put a hand on my arm. 'I hope you find them,' she said.

'I think I'll find them,' I told her. 'I just hope I'm not too late.'

There was a long silence.

'What are you going to do after you've found him?'

I shrugged. 'No idea.'

'No job yet?'

'No.'

'Are you going to specialise? Get another hospital job?'

I shook my head. 'I'll find a general practice locum while I look around.'

'You'll make a good GP,' she said. 'You always treat the patients like people. Not everyone does.'

I felt embarrassed. 'You run the best ward in the business,' I told her. I believed it. It was probably true.

'We'll miss you,' she said suddenly. She stood up and kissed me on the lips. 'I'll miss you,' she said, emphasising the 'I'. There was a tear in her left eye. She wiped it away angrily. 'You young doctors are always buggering off and leaving us,' she said accusingly. 'You come here like larvae and fly off as butterflies.' She frowned. 'Is it larvae or pupae?'

I shrugged and smiled at her. 'Dunno.'

'Look after yourself.'

'And you. And thanks for everything.'

'I won't promise to write or anything because I won't. I never get time to write letters. Anyway I'm a rotten bloody correspondent. I can never think of anything to say.'

'No.'

'So bugger off now. I've got work to do.'

I buggered off.

# CHAPTER 3

I knew why Henry had gone. I knew who'd pushed his wheelchair. And I knew why he'd taken the nitrazepam. I just didn't know where to find him.

I carried the plastic bag containing his meagre belongings to the doctors' mess where I'd left my suitcase and my bag. I crammed the whole lot in the boot of my battered old Humber and went back into the mess to telephone the RAC. There was no point in even trying to start the car because the battery had been flat when I'd last tried it.

'Your battery is gone,' said the RAC patrolman, after he'd started my car with his jump leads. I hid my surprise well. 'There isn't enough juice in it to power one of those little torches you guys use to look down people's throats. I don't know where you're going but I suggest that before you go there you visit a garage and treat yourself to a new one.'

'How much are they?'

He told me.

'Know anywhere cheap?'

He sighed and grinned. 'I thought you doctors were all loaded.'

'Just take a good look at the car,' I told him.

He gave me the address of a garage. 'And get them to put a bit of air in the tyres,' he suggested. 'You're driving on the rims.'

I said I would. 'And you stop smoking and lose some weight.'
He laughed, climbed back into his van and sped off.

★★★

The visit to the garage would have to wait. I needed to find
Henry and his wife, Daphne. After Henry's admission to hospital
he had arranged for the caravan his wife lived in to be moved to a
small private site no more than a mile and a half from the hospital.
It was close enough for Daphne to walk to the hospital for both
afternoon and evening visiting. Visiting time was 3 pm to 4 pm
in the afternoons and 7.30 pm to 8 pm in the evenings. Daphne
never missed. She walked six miles a day to be with her husband
every minute that she could. I had first visited the caravan in a
thunderstorm. Daphne had been about to walk home at 8 pm after
the evening's half hour visiting time was over. I would have taken
her home in my car but I knew it wouldn't start so I persuaded one
of the ambulance drivers to take her home. I went with them to
make sure she got home safely. In return for this favour I prescribed
something appropriate for an embarrassing condition the ambulance
driver had picked up and didn't want anyone to know about.

★★★

The caravan, parked at the edge of a site consisting of thirty or
forty vans, looked empty. The door was locked and the curtains
were drawn. I got out of the car, leaving the engine running, and
banged on the caravan door. No one answered. I walked round and
peered inside through a gap in the curtains. Everything looked very
clean. And empty. I heard my car's engine stop running.

'She's gone,' said a voice.

I turned round.

A woman who had clearly either heard me knocking or seen
me arrive was standing in the doorway of her own caravan just ten
or twelve yards away. She wore a thick knitted cardigan that came
down to her knees and a knitted skirt. Both were multi-coloured
and looked as if they had been made up of odds and ends of wool.
Her hair was long and matted and clearly hadn't been washed for
a long, long time.

'Do you know when she went?'

'She went out at about six yesterday evening and didn't come back.'

Two small children, I couldn't tell the sexes, appeared behind her legs. They both had long blond hair and were sucking lollipops. Their faces and clothes were filthy. One of them scratched constantly. A mangy looking mongrel appeared, obviously having just woken up. It saw me and barked and growled. When it got fed up with barking and growling it began to lick and scratch itself.

'I expect she went to the hospital. I don't suppose you know where she went to after that?'

'No idea.'

'Do you have a telephone?'

She laughed. 'Telephone? Me?' She shook her head. 'No, love.'

'I need to ring the RAC to start my car.'

'There's a public telephone box over there,' she said, pointing. I turned, thanked her and headed towards the box. The dog was growling and barking again but it was too fond of licking and scratching to put its heart into it.

'Come and see me if you want a cup of tea while you wait,' the woman shouted. I waved a hand in thanks.

The telephone box had the stink common to telephone boxes everywhere. I called the RAC and went back to the car. I sat in the passenger seat and waited for them to arrive. The dog had now given up barking and growling completely and was devoting itself full-time to licking and scratching. The woman and the children had disappeared, presumably back into the caravan. I hoped the woman wouldn't think too badly of me for ignoring her offer. I studied the car manual so that it looked as if I was busy reading something important. It was just that I didn't want to catch the fleas with which her children and dog were obviously infested. The manual was very boring and I didn't understand much of it. But I did find out how to turn the fog lights on which was something of a bonus since I'd been trying to find out how to do that ever since I'd bought the car.

★★★

When the car was running I drove to the garage the first mechanic had recommended and bought a new battery. I had to put my own air in the tyres. Ninety minutes later, the old Humber refreshed, and my wallet not as much lighter as I had feared, I drove into town to find somewhere to sleep for a few nights while I decided what to do next. Smart hotels were obviously out so I was looking for somewhere cheap, clean and cheerful. A boarding house would do. Somewhere that I could sleep, bathe, and dump my case while trying to figure out what to do next.

Before Amanda had worked out our prospective incomes and had dumped me for the estate agent with the better potential I had planned to consider my future while lying on a beach or by the hotel swimming pool. I'd thought I might take a copy of the British Medical Journal with me and look through the advertisements at the back of the magazine. I would, at least, have had somewhere to eat and sleep while I pondered my future. The abandoning of the holiday had left me with the British Medical Journal but no hotel and no beach.

But finding a job could wait for a few days while I tried to find Henry and Daphne Mulligan. As far as that was concerned the cancelling of the holiday had been a boon. I wondered what I would have done if Amanda hadn't cancelled our relationship. Would I have abandoned the holiday so that I could search for Henry? I knew I would. It was, perhaps, a good job that Amanda had cancelled first.

There were some things I knew for sure. And some things I didn't know. I went through them in my mind.

1. I knew why Henry had gone.
2. I knew Daphne had gone with him (pushing the wheelchair).
3. I didn't know where they had gone.
4. I knew I didn't have long to find them.
5. Most important of all, I knew I had to find them. I wanted to say 'goodbye'. I owed Henry that much.

# CHAPTER 4

Henry and Daphne were devoted to one another. They had met when he was eighteen and she was fifteen. And they'd married a year later.

'We've never spent a day apart,' he told me. 'Until I had to come into the hospital we'd never spent a night apart.'

He loved to talk about her.

'She was very pretty,' he said. 'I think she's very pretty now, but when she was a young girl men always used to turn to look at her. I was never jealous though. Proud, I suppose. And pleased for her. Do you think women like being admired?'

'I don't know,' I said.

'I would imagine they do,' said Henry. 'I think I would if I were a woman.'

★★★

In 1917, just sixteen years old, Henry had joined the army. He hadn't lost his thumb in an industrial accident as the medical examiner had said during my finals, though that was what Henry often told people. He'd lost it in Ypres when it had been shot off by a German bullet which had smashed his hand against the stock of his rifle.

'Why don't you tell people the truth about it?' I asked him one day.

He had shrugged. 'People aren't interested in that war,' he said. 'It embarrasses them. The young don't know anything about it. I just want to forget it.'

'Did you get a disability pension?' I asked him.

'I was supposed to get one,' he said. 'No more than a few bob. But I never got a penny. The paperwork never got through. And I didn't like to ask about it. There were a lot who were much worse off than I was.'

★★★

Daphne had something that was then known as senile dementia. And her condition was deteriorating rapidly.

She had visited Henry ever since he'd first been brought into the hospital but recently she'd started getting lost and people had noticed.

The police had twice found her wandering along a nearby dual carriageway and they'd told the social workers. As a result social workers were planning to move Daphne from her caravan and put her into a council run nursing home for the disturbed and demented. I had been there when I was a medical student. It was a dismal and depressing place; woefully understaffed and poorly financed. It was more like an offshoot of a 19th century poorhouse or workhouse than a 20th century hospital. In the daytime the patients sat around on red plastic chairs and stared at one another. There were so few staff members that all the patients were heavily sedated. No one spoke. No one went out. And the whole place was so darkly depressing that hardly anyone visited. Friends and relatives would call once or twice but then find excellent reasons why they couldn't call again. There were patients in that place who hadn't seen (or been seen by) a soul they knew for years. 'Will you take me to the hospital to see my husband?' was the first thing Daphne asked when the social workers told her what they were planning.

'We'll try and fix up someone to take you over but it won't be every day,' the social workers told her.

'How often will it be?' she asked them.

'Maybe once a month or so,' they had lied.

But she was demented not stupid and she knew that they were lying. She cried so much that when she saw Henry the next day he knew instantly that something was wrong. He made her tell him.

# MR HENRY MULLIGAN

★★★

When I could I used to take Daphne home to her caravan from the hospital. She was no more than five feet tall and couldn't have weighed more than seven stone. She was like a living doll. She loved brightly coloured clothes and always dressed smartly, albeit eccentrically. 'I don't want to let my Henry down,' she told me time and time again. When she arrived at the hospital after her long walk from their caravan she would slip into the ladies' to tidy her hair and refresh her make up. Daphne and I had often talked together. She was a fascinating and well-read woman who knew an enormous amount about a wide range of subjects. Like Henry's father, she had taught herself to read and write. And once she'd learned to read she had never stopped reading. And never stopped learning. She knew far more about English history than anyone else I'd ever met. And she had studied nature extensively. She didn't always know what day of the week it was, she couldn't tell you the name of the Prime Minister and she couldn't subtract seven from a hundred but she could identify every tree, every bird and every flower we passed.

But her favourite subject was, without a doubt, her Henry. She loved him, worshipped him and adored him. No woman could have loved a man more.

Long after she was officially diagnosed as demented she had moments of great lucidity.

'Henry is a gentleman and a very proud man,' she had told me once. He was down at the X-ray department having another check up. 'We got on a train once,' she remembered. 'About two years ago. We were going to Leeds. Or it may have been Reading.' She shook her head. 'I can't remember where it was. Or why. There were five empty seats when we got on.' She stopped and thought for a moment. 'It wasn't Leeds or Reading,' she said. 'It wasn't a train. It was a bus in Chingford. Four young men got on with us. They all wore green anoraks. Those ugly jackets they sell in the army stores. Lots of pockets and buttons. But they weren't soldiers. They were very loud. They were laughing a lot and drinking beer from cans. They pushed their way past us and they all sat down. Henry wanted me to sit down in the seat that was left but he was so ill I knew he couldn't stand all that way. I made him take the remaining seat. He so much wanted me to sit down.' Tears appeared in her eyes as she remembered. 'He knew he couldn't stand,' she said. 'He had a stick but he shouldn't have been walking.' She lowered her voice and beckoned a finger, indicating that I should move closer so that she could whisper. 'He has a weak heart you know.'

'I know,' I said gently.

'Of course you do,' she said quietly, with a faint smile. 'You're the doctor aren't you.'

I nodded.

'He was so ashamed,' she continued. 'He cried. The four young men saw him and they pointed at him and laughed. Henry made me get off at the next stop even though it wasn't the right one for us. We stood in the rain and waited another forty minutes for the next bus. He got a bad chest infection and was ill for months afterwards. We never went out after that. He's never really been the same again.'

She stopped and thought for a while. 'We never went out after that,' she repeated.

There was another long pause while she thought about what had happened.

'They were very cruel,' she said. 'Why would people do that?'

'I don't know,' I confessed. I blinked, trying to hold back the tears, and shook my head. 'I don't know, Mrs Mulligan.'

'He was in the war, you know,' she said to me.

'I know,' I said.

'He was a hero,' she said. 'My Henry was a war hero. But he doesn't talk about it. He doesn't tell anyone.'

'I know,' I said. 'He had his thumb shot off.'

She looked at me, puzzled. 'Oh that,' she said at last. 'Oh yes, there was the thumb.' She paused. 'But that was a long, long time ago.'

At the time I didn't understand.

Only later did I realise that Daphne and I had been talking about different wars.

★★★

One day it was raining hard and I knew Daphne would get soaked if she walked to the hospital. I arranged for another doctor to cover me for a few minutes in the hospital and I drove out to her caravan to pick her up. When I got there I leapt out of the car and stood on her doorstep banging on the door. But there was no answer. I stood there in the pouring rain. I felt sure that Daphne was inside.

'Daphne!' I called. 'I've come to take you to see Henry. It's pouring down. If you don't come with me you'll get soaked.'

But still she wouldn't open the door.

Somehow I knew she was in there. I got into my car and drove fifty yards away and stopped. It was raining so hard that at that distance I could hardly see the caravan. I knew she could hardly see my car either.

I parked in such a way that I could watch the path coming from her caravan. Sure enough, after five minutes or so Daphne appeared. She was wearing a thin summer dress. The dress was coloured light blue but most of it was already dark blue because of the rain. I opened the passenger door as she came level with the car.

'Daphne,' I said, 'it's me. Can I give you a lift to the hospital?'

She smiled at me and got into the car without hesitation. 'That's nice of you,' she said. 'It's raining.'

'Why didn't you open the caravan door to me?' I asked her as we drove to the hospital.

'Henry always tells me never to open the door to anyone,' she said. 'He never opens the door either.'

I laughed. It sounded just like Henry. 'Why not?'

'Henry says that there is never any point in opening the door if you're not expecting visitors,' she explained. 'He says that when there is someone at the door unexpectedly it is always someone who wants something from you and never someone who wants to do something for you.'

'That's very true,' I admitted, still laughing. 'Very wise.'

I could just hear Henry saying that.

★★★

I was sitting by Henry's bedside. We were finishing the crossword in the Daily Mail. We neither of us read the Daily Mail but we often used to do the crossword. It was easier than the ones in most of the other papers. A woman in a grey suit approached us. She ignored me. 'Henry?' she said. She was carrying a clipboard. She didn't wait for a reply. 'I'm Mrs Cuthbertson,' she said. 'I need to ask you a few questions.'

'My name is Mr Mulligan,' said Henry.

'I beg your pardon?' said the woman.

'My name is Mulligan,' said Henry. 'Henry Mulligan.'

'I'm from social services administration,' said the woman. She tried to smile but she wasn't very good at it. She seemed confused.

'What's your Christian name?' Henry asked her.

'I beg your pardon?'

'If we're going to be on first name terms I need to know your first name,' said Henry politely.

The woman didn't understand. I smiled to myself. It was, Henry had once said, just a question of respect. 'If you start off a relationship without respect you'll never acquire it,' Henry once said.

'Maybe I should do this some other time,' said the woman nervously.

'No, you can do it now,' said Henry.

'We think your wife needs to be taken into special care,' said the woman in the grey suit. 'She's become very confused and we think she's a danger to herself.'

'Have you spoken to her?'

'She asked us to speak to you,' said the woman.

'Does she want to go into special care?'

'She said she wanted to stay in the caravan,' said the woman. 'But I'm afraid that's really not possible.'

'Why not?'

'Well, your wife is very confused. We arranged for one of our trained mental health workers to visit her. She wouldn't let him in. He felt that she would be safer if offered institutional care. We have reports from the police showing that on at least two separate occasions your wife has been found wandering.'

'If she wants to stay in the caravan then that's where I want her to stay,' said Henry firmly. 'If she wanders the police can take her home, can't they?'

'I'm afraid that's not possible,' said the grey suited woman. 'We have the authority to take your wife into care and that's what we think is necessary.'

Henry looked at me. He looked tired. 'Can they do that?'

I nodded. 'I'm afraid so,' I said.

'I really came to give you formal notice of our intentions,' said the woman.

'Will she be able to come and visit me?' asked Henry. 'I won't be able to visit her.'

'We will do our best to arrange something. Perhaps once a month might be possible.'

Henry swallowed. He and Daphne had never spent a day apart. I knew that neither he nor she would cope well if they were separated.

'It isn't possible for me to live in this place with her?'

'Oh good heavens no,' said the woman. 'There aren't any facilities for caring for physically disabled patients. This is a specialised unit for the mentally ill. Very special types of mental illness.'

'So we don't really have a choice?'

'Well, if you put it that way...' said the woman. She seemed uncomfortable.

'You're going to lock my wife up so that we can't see one another?'

'No, it's not like that at all...'

'What's it like then?'

'There isn't much point in our continuing like this,' said the woman, lifting her head and sticking out her chin. She seemed offended.

'When's it going to happen?' I asked.

The woman looked at me. It was as though it was the first time she'd noticed me. 'And you are?'

'I'm Mr Mulligan's doctor.'

The woman was flustered and started to redden. 'Oh, I didn't know you were a doctor,' she said. 'I thought you were a porter... or something.' She looked at me as though she didn't really believe that I was a doctor. I'd been up all night trying (and failing) to save a road accident victim. I hadn't shaved. I hadn't washed or changed either. I had blood stains on my shirt and my white coat.

'When is it going to happen?' I asked again.

'A week on Wednesday,' said the woman. 'A week on Wednesday, Mr Mulligan,' she said, putting a lot of emphasis on the Mr. 'Have a nice day, Mr Mulligan,' she added.

'I usually have whatever sort of day God gives me,' said Henry. 'And it seems like he's giving me a pretty shitty day today.'

The woman looked at him, looked at me, and then marched off, holding her clipboard under her arm.

★★★

'I don't think she liked us,' I said, when she'd disappeared from the ward.

'Who cares?' asked Henry. 'It doesn't matter what people you don't know or care about think of you. All that matters is what you and the people whom you care about think of you.' He stared in the direction the woman had taken. 'Bastards,' he muttered. 'They're all bastards.'

'I'm sorry,' I said.

'What sort of place is this,' asked Henry. 'The one where they're going to send Daphne.'

'It's a specialist home for people who are confused,' I told him.

'What's it like?'

'Very nice lawn. Red plastic armchairs. Plastic furniture. Locks on the doors.'

'Full of nutters?'

'I don't think that's the term they use these days.'

'Daphne's not nutty,' said Henry. 'She's just a bit forgetful.'

'The police found her wandering along the dual carriageway the other day,' I reminded him. 'It was raining. She was wearing her nightie and a pair of slippers.'

'She wanted to buy some milk to make me a bread and butter pudding,' explained Henry. 'She got a bit lost that's all.'

'It's easily done,' I agreed.

'Why do they do that?' he asked. 'Why do they put all the confused people in one place. It's really stupid.'

'I suppose it's so that they can keep an eye on them,' I said.

'They do it with depressed patients,' said Henry. He looked down at the crossword we had nearly completed, and now never would. 'I had an aunt once who was depressed. She's long gone now, bless her, but they put her in a hospital ward that was chock full of depressed patients. There must have been thirty people in there. All depressed. Not a smile in the place. I used to visit her. When I came out it took me days to recover. The staff were all depressed too.'

'I see your point,' I admitted.

'If they put Daphne in a home with lots of other people who are confused she'll get worse and worse,' said Henry. He thought for a long, long moment. 'They won't let her out, will they?'

'Not by herself,' I agreed, softly. It was breaking his heart and it was breaking mine too. I had seen them together. Separating them seemed so very, very cruel.

'And they say they'll bring her to see me but they won't.'

'Oh, I'm sure...'

He looked at me.

I sighed deeply. 'No,' I admitted after a long pause. 'No, they probably won't.'

'So she'll quietly rot away in their home. And I'll quietly rot here.'

I didn't say anything. I couldn't think of anything worthwhile to say.

'I don't suppose we have any choice?'

'About Daphne going into the home?'

He nodded.

'No,' I said. 'If the forms have been signed then I'm afraid there isn't any choice. They'll take her there whether she agrees or not. You can't stop them. Nor can I.'

'I thought so,' said Henry. 'They're like the bloody Gestapo.'

He didn't speak for a while. Neither of us did. Then Henry sighed. It was as though all the breath was coming out of him. 'Health doesn't matter at all until you notice it and then it's the only thing that does matter,' he said wearily.

He suddenly seemed very, very old.

★★★

The white coats that doctors wear have large patch pockets into which all sorts of things can be crammed. That evening I bought half a bottle of malt whisky and stuffed it into one of my white coat pockets. I put two drinking glasses into the other pocket. I got one of the nurses to help me lift Henry into a wheelchair and I took him into the deserted day room.

'This is medicinal,' I said, taking out the whisky and the two glasses.

'Are you prescribing it?' he asked. He picked up the bottle, examined the label and made an approving face.

'I certainly am,' I said.

Just then one of the more pompous nurses came in and saw us. 'Is Mr Mulligan supposed to be drinking whisky, doctor?' she asked, rather sternly.

'I'm not sure,' I said. 'Would you be kind enough to bring in his drug sheet?' She went away and, a moment or two later, returned with Henry's official prescription records. She handed the records to me. 'I don't think I can see whisky on there, doctor,' she said.

I took out a pen and wrote 'Whisky as required' on the sheet. Then I signed it and handed it back to her. 'Look again,' I said. She left us.

'I wish you could sort out Daphne's damned social workers that easily,' said Henry.

'Me too,' I said.

I poured us both a drink.

★★★

We talked about death. I asked him if he'd regretted having been a smoker. He smiled and shook his head.

'Somewhere in Ghana,' he told me, 'there's a tribe which believes that none of us dies a natural death. They believe that every death is a murder and for every victim there is someone to hold responsible.'

'So if everyone who dies is a victim how do they deal with all the murderers?' I asked.

'The tribe use magic to find out who killed the man who died.

Then, when the murderer has been identified, the dead man's oldest son is given his father's sandals to keep. When the son is big enough to wear his father's sandals it is his duty to avenge his father's death by killing the man who has been convicted of his father's murder.'

'And then the son...'

He nodded. 'The son of the newly murdered man is given his father's sandals. When he grows old enough...and so the cycle of murder continues. The tribe's whole structure is built upon blame and revenge.'

'But you don't blame the cigarettes?'

'Who cares about the cigarettes? It's myself I don't blame,' he said. 'You're a doctor,' he went on. 'You must know that non-smokers can die of lung cancer too.'

I nodded.

'So I cannot know the cigarettes were to blame.'

'No. But...'

'And so I don't have to blame myself.'

Understanding, I nodded.

'We might think the people in that African tribe are primitive,' he said. 'But we're becoming just as bad. I know people who are always looking for someone to blame if something goes wrong in their life.'

I nodded.

'In ten or twenty years time,' he said, 'lawyers will be advertising for clients who want to sue. Everyone will want to blame someone for everything bad that happens to them. The pedestrian who trips will sue the council. The man who falls off a ladder will sue the man who made the ladder – or the man who sold it to him.'

I thought he was exaggerating to make a point. I said so.

'Perhaps,' he laughed. 'You'll be alive to know. I won't.'

We both knew he was dying. And he was doing it faster than most of us.

But there was something in the way he talked about his dying that stayed with me.

# CHAPTER 5

I rented a room in a small hotel near the railway station. It called itself a hotel and insofar as it was a place providing rooms and meals for travellers and tourists no one could really argue with that description. But if, when you think of hotels, you think of flowers in the lobby, polite reception staff, willing porters, well-polished brass doorknobs, crisp white sheets, chocolates on the pillows and fluffy white towels in the bathroom then you are not thinking of Mrs Potter's establishment.

My bed had chocolate on the pillow but it wasn't a chocolate disk neatly wrapped in gold foil and presented with the compliments of the management. The chocolate on my pillow was merely a smear, left over from some previous occupant's night-time snack.

It was a long time since the solitary towel hanging on a wobbly plastic rail screwed to the wall beside my sink had ever been fluffy, a long time since the white plastic door handle had been wiped and, I suspected, a long, long time since Mrs Potter had smiled at one of her guests. The bathroom was down the hall and if I wanted to use it I had to ask Mrs Potter for the key. I was, according to a notice hanging by her shabby cubby hole, allowed one bath a day without extra charge. The only furniture in the room was a cheap wardrobe, a single bed and a bedside table. There was no bedside lamp. The floor was covered with a thin mat which looked as though it needed a good shake.

Still, it was somewhere to stay, it was cheap and, to my surprise, there was a small patch of wasteland round the back of the hotel where I could leave my car.

I crammed my luggage, unopened, in the tiny, rickety wardrobe, turned the pillow over to hide the chocolate stain, jammed the rattling window (which, conveniently enough, gave me a view of the patch of wasteland and, therefore, a chance to keep an occasional eye on my car) and sat down on the bed with the plastic bag which contained Henry's belongings.

I carefully tipped the contents out onto the pink candlewick bedspread. First, I sorted out the clothes (a blue shirt, a pair of striped pyjamas, a couple of pairs of socks and a few sets of underclothing) and put them back into the bag. Then I examined what was left.

There was a paperback copy of Three Men In A Boat by Jerome K.Jerome, a large brown envelope which was sealed and a packet of photographs which was unsealed.

I took the photographs out of the envelope. All the photographs were black and white. The top photograph was of a young couple. The man, clearly Henry, was wearing a suit and a trilby hat. The woman was wearing a flowered dress and was carrying a small bucket and spade; the sort of implements children use to dig with on a sandy beach. They were on a beach. And between them, sitting on a donkey, there was a boy dressed only in bathing trunks. To one side, standing alone, was another woman. She looked full of sadness. I didn't know who she was. Maybe the wife of the photographer?

Who was the boy?

He looked too old to be their son. He must have been ten or eleven. It was difficult to tell how old Henry and Daphne were, but they didn't look old enough to have a son of that age. And yet the boy looked just like Henry. He had to be their son.

I flicked through the other photographs. One was of a younger Henry and Daphne. They were sitting on a sea wall holding hands. I turned the photograph over. On the back was printed the name and address of a photographer. Someone had written. 'Honeymoon. Second Day.' on the back in pencil.

★★★

I remembered something that had happened months earlier. Henry and I had been sitting in the day room. It had been about four o'clock in the morning. I'd been to the ward to put a catheter into an old man who'd got urinary retention and, afterwards, I'd found Henry reading a John Buchan novel. He didn't much care for the books they had on the hospital library trolley and Daphne brought him in paperbacks she'd found for him in charity shops.

'I wish I could have been more of a husband to Daphne,' Henry had said.

'What on earth do you mean?' I had asked him. 'Daphne adores you.'

'I wish we could have had children of our own,' he'd said. There had been a long pause. 'But that side of our marriage wasn't as strong as I would have liked it to be.' He had stared into space for a long, long time. 'She was always faithful to me, though,' he had said, at last.

I knew what Henry was talking about. I'd examined him enough times.

★★★

I looked through the rest of the photographs but there were no more photographs of a boy. If he hadn't looked so much like Henry I would have wondered if it had been a friend's child. Maybe even the son of a couple they'd met on holiday and were looking after for an hour or two. But the boy had Henry's eyes and Henry's nose. He looked exactly like Henry.

★★★

Mrs Potter said she didn't serve meals apart from breakfast. So I drove back to the hospital, went into the canteen and bought a salad and a bowl of spotted dick with custard. The salad was warm, the spotted dick had very few spots and the custard somehow managed to be both weak and lumpy but it was food, it filled me up and it was cheap. I saw quite a few people I knew but no one thought it in the slightest bit odd that I was eating there. The ones who knew I had finished my last contract probably just thought I'd taken another job in the hospital. Anyone who knew I hadn't probably realised I was just solving two problems (hunger and poverty) in the easiest way. After I'd eaten I went back to the ward. I was lucky – Sister Tomkins, the ward sister was on a late shift.

'Did anyone ever visit Henry Mulligan when he was a patient here?' I asked. 'Apart from his wife.' I added.

She thought for a moment. 'Just his wife,' she said. 'I never saw anyone else visit.'

'No other relatives?'

Sister Tomkins thought and shook her head. 'I wish I knew how he'd got away,' she said. 'I still feel terrible about it. I've never lost a patient before.'

'It wasn't your fault,' I told her. 'He went in his wheelchair.'

'But he didn't have the strength to wheel himself.'

'No. But his wife did. Daphne.'

'You think Daphne wheeled him out of here?'

'Yes. She often used to wheel him out into the rose garden in the afternoon. He'd direct her and she'd push. She was a bit confused but she was used to walking and she was stronger than she looked.'

'But why? Why would he go?'

'The social workers were going to put Daphne into a nursing home,' I explained. 'Some sort of place for patients with dementia. They told her that they'd bring her to see Henry once a month.'

'I can see that not going down well.'

'Neither of them would accept that,' I said. 'So they had to leave.'

'But where?' asked Sister Tomkins. 'Where on earth would they go? What sort of future could they possibly have out there in the big wide nasty world? Two sick people with no money and no prospects.'

'I don't know where they've gone,' I said. 'But I'm going to try and find them.' I didn't tell her that I knew what sort of future they had. 'Do you know if they had a son?' I asked.

Sister Tomkins thought for a moment, then shook her head. 'I don't think so.'

'Do you still have Henry's medical notes?'

Sister Tomkins looked around her tiny office. 'They should have gone down to Medical Records by now,' she said. She reached into an overstuffed filing tray and sorted through the mass of papers it contained. 'But they haven't.' She handed me the file.

'Can I borrow this?'

'What on earth do you want that for?'

'Maybe there will be a clue in here that will help me find them.'

'I can't let you take medical records. They're hospital property.'

I looked through the office window. 'Mr Reynolds looks as if his pillows need plumping up a bit,' I said.

Sister Tomkins looked at him, then looked at me. 'You're right,' she said. 'They do.' She got up and headed for the door. 'I expect you'll be gone when I get back.'

'I expect I will,' I said.

I was. And so, oddly enough, were Henry's medical records.

★★★

I drove back to my hotel, parked the car and went up to my room. The bits and pieces of Henry's life which I had left on my bed were still there. I sat down on the edge of the bed and opened up Henry's medical records. I didn't bother with the last part of the file. I had written most of it myself and knew there was nothing there that would be of any help. I was interested only in the first few pages, the admission notes that had been written when Henry Mulligan had first come into the hospital. I had been a medical student then, of course.

The house officer who had admitted Henry to the hospital had done a thorough job. In addition to performing an extensive physical examination that must have taken the best part of an hour to complete he had also made full notes about Henry's past personal, social and medical history. It was the personal and social history that I was looking for.

According to the admission notes Henry and Daphne had married in 1919. There was no record of Henry's war service. And there was no record of the couple having had any children. In fact, the doctor writing the admission notes had specifically asked about children. And Henry had said he didn't have any.

But there was a brother.

Could the boy in the photograph have been Henry's brother?

The doctor hadn't bothered to make a note of a birth date for the brother so the boy in the photograph could have been a brother. It would have explained the fact that he looked just like Henry. Maybe Henry and his young bride had taken his young brother to the seaside on holiday.

If Henry had a younger brother there would be a good chance that he was still alive. If I could find him I might find Henry and Daphne.

I looked again through the photographs I had. Most of the photographs were of Henry and Daphne. There were no other photographs of anyone who could be a younger brother.

I took everything off the eiderdown and placed it carefully on the floor. Except for the paperback. I put that on the bedside table. I undressed, washed, got into bed, opened Henry's copy of Three Men in a Boat and was so tired I fell asleep before I had read a page of it.

★★★

When I woke the following morning the light was on. I had left it on all night. Henry's copy of Three Men In A Boat was lying on the floor face open where it had fallen. A piece of paper was on the floor beside the book.

I got out of bed and found my shoes. The carpet was gritty with dirt. Walking on it in bare feet was like walking on a sandy beach. Then I picked up the book and the piece of paper that had fallen out of it.

The paper, which Henry had presumably been using as a bookmark, was a pawn ticket. I examined it carefully. There were two days left in which to redeem whatever had been pawned. There was a number on the ticket but no description of what had been pawned and no details of any other kind. The shop which had issued the ticket was within easy walking distance of the hotel. I wondered how Henry had managed to visit a pawn shop. Then I realised that Daphne must have done it for him. They must have needed money. But what had they pawned?

I now had two leads to follow up.

The missing brother and the pawn ticket.

I washed, shaved, dressed and went downstairs to breakfast. The tiny dining room was empty. I looked at the clock. It was ten to nine. I sat down at the only table that had been cleared.

'Continental or cooked?' asked a girl of about sixteen who appeared, as though by magic. She was wearing a waitress uniform that was several sizes too big for her and was carrying a small notepad and a pencil.

'Sorry?'

'Do you want continental or cooked breakfast?'

'What's the continental breakfast?'

'French toast and coffee.'

'I'll have the cooked breakfast, please.'

'Full English?'

'Yes, please.'

'Tea or coffee?'

'Tea, please.'

'White or brown?'

'White or brown tea?'

'Toast.'

'Oh, brown, please.'

'Room number?'

I told her. She disappeared as mysteriously as she had appeared. I heard her shout my order to someone in the kitchen. Moments later she reappeared carrying a metal teapot and a tiny jug of milk. 'Sugar and cups are on the sideboard,' she told me before disappearing again. I couldn't see where she went. I fetched a cup and saucer and poured myself a cup of stewed tea. Five minutes later she reappeared carrying a white plate upon which lay a puddle of fat in which, like small islands, lay a blackened rasher of bacon, half a fried tomato, a mushroom, an overfried egg and a spoonful of baked beans. She used a teatowel to protect her hands from the hot plate. 'Watch the plate,' she instructed. 'It's hot.' She disappeared, but I didn't see how or where she went.

I was hungry and young so I apologised to my stomach and my

arteries and ate it all. I tried to leave as much of the fat on the plate as I could.

I had finished my breakfast and had stood up and was about to leave when a young woman swept in. She was tall and slim and had shoulder length blonde hair. She wore a mini skirt that seemed little wider than a decent belt, a skin tight sweater that sparkled and a pair of high-heeled shoes that added five inches to her height. She glanced at me, looked around then sat down at the table I'd just vacated. The waitress came in and looked at the clock rather pointedly.

'Coffee and toast, please, Elsie' said the newcomer. The waitress wrote it down and disappeared.

I too disappeared. But at least I knew which door I went through.

★★★

'I'd like to redeem this,' I said sliding the pawn ticket through a gap to the man on the other side of a thick metal grille. The man behind the grille was bald and wore a gold earring in his left ear. I'd never seen a man with an earring before. It was a large earring and gave him a jaunty, piratical air. He took the ticket and checked the number on the ticket against a list of numbers in a large black leather bound ledger.

'Sixty pounds,' he told me. He said it as though it wasn't anything very special.

I stared at him in astonishment. I'd been paid very little more than that for a month's work at the hospital.

'Do you want to redeem it or not?' demanded the man, impatiently.

I thought about asking him what 'it' was but decided against it. If he knew I didn't know what I was trying to redeem he might assume that I had stolen the ticket.

'I'll come back later,' I said.

He pushed the ticket back under the grille and I put it into my wallet.

I couldn't imagine what Henry could have owned that would have been worth so much money.

And I couldn't imagine where I was going to get £60 so

that I could find out what it was. It might as well have been £6,000,000.

★★★

I walked back to the hotel and once again went through the stuff Henry had left behind. I tore open the brown envelope. I didn't have a kettle so couldn't steam the flap open. I tipped the contents out onto the bed.

There was a small, battered, dark blue address book, some postcards and a small sheaf of newspaper cuttings clipped together with an ordinary pin.

I opened the address book first. Most of the entries had been crossed out, with a single red line drawn neatly through the name and the letters RIP written at the end of the line. Henry and Daphne had, it seemed, lived longer than most of their friends. Most of the remaining entries were tradesmen and so on. A plumber, electrician, handyman, television repair engineer and heating engineer. There was the name of a general practitioner and details of a dental surgery. There were addresses and telephone numbers for three hotels and one or two caravan parks. Most of these were in Devon. Amidst all the sad crossings out there were just two addresses for real people. One was an address in Australia with, beside it, the added note, 'Daphne's niece. Birthday 3.8.53. The other was someone called George Pardoe who had an address just a few miles away in Worcester.

The messages on the postcards weren't very exciting and didn't seem to get me anywhere. One card just had the words 'Always yours and thinking of you all the time' written on it. A second contained the words 'My love is yours forever. The third just had 'I love you darling. Keep safe for me.' They were all addressed to Henry and signed by Daphne. She had neat, very feminine handwriting and she had added three kisses to each of the cards. She'd made them very small and neat and I could imagine that she had been embarrassed at sending them through the mail on a postcard. But not so embarrassed that she would not put them there.

I picked up the newspaper cuttings. One of the clippings, dating from 1943, contained a picture of a soldier holding up a medal. 'Local Born Soldier Receives Gallantry Medal' ran the headline. The story described how Private Michael Mulligan had been awarded the George Medal for bravery.

'Private Mulligan was returning to his unit at the end of a three day pass when the rear part of the train in which he was travelling was hit by a German flying bomb. Private Mulligan, who was travelling in the coach immediately behind the engine risked his life by repeatedly entering the train and rescuing passengers.'

'Because the incident occurred a mile and a half from the nearest road the emergency services had difficulty in reaching the scene of the disaster. Private Mulligan, acting alone, rescued an elderly man, two women, three children and a baby from certain death. He ignored the danger to his own person in doing this.'

'When the emergency services finally arrived at the scene, Private Mulligan was able to direct them to those areas of the wreckage where passengers were still trapped.'

'The George Medal is usually awarded to citizens but was awarded to Private Mulligan because, in this instance, he was acting in a personal capacity rather than as a member of His Majesty's Armed Forces.'

A second cutting was a report of a Parliamentary By Election in which Michael Mulligan, the Labour candidate for the constituency, had been unsuccessful. The report included a few lines describing how Mr Mulligan had shed a few tears when thanking his party workers in his post-election address.

★★★

I had one possibly useful lead: the address of George Pardoe. Since he hadn't yet had a line drawn through his name I hoped that he was still alive.

I didn't know what to make of any of it so I picked up the photographs again. The only one that seemed relevant was still the one showing Henry, Daphne and the unknown boy. Fed up of staring at the photograph and learning nothing more from it I turned it over and looked at the back. There was faded writing scrawled just underneath the top edge. It was obviously some sort of description of the contents of the photograph. I took the photograph over to the window and peered closely at it. The caption had been written in thick, soft pencil but it was just about readable. There were three names, written in a flowing, soft, feminine handwriting.

'Henry, Michael and Daphne.'

So the boy on the donkey was called Michael.

But was he Daphne and Henry's son? Or was he Henry's brother?

And would he know where Henry and Daphne might be?

And how could I find him?

All I knew about him was that he had received a medal for bravery during the Second World War.

At least, that was what I thought I knew. I was to learn that in Henry's life things weren't always quite what they seemed.

# CHAPTER 6

There was a knock on my door. It was my landlady.

'There's an urgent call for you,' she announced. She handed me a piece of paper with a number written on it. 'You're to phone Dr Taylor as soon as possible,' she said. She had a sharp, strident voice with a pronounced Birmingham accent.

I looked at the paper she'd given me. There was nothing written on it but the telephone number. I tried, but failed, to think of a Dr Taylor I might know. 'Do you know what he wants?' I asked.

'No,' said the landlady. She looked at me sternly. 'You haven't got a nasty infectious disease, have you?'

'Not that I know of,' I said.

'He could be public health,' said the landlady. 'I've never heard of doctors ringing patients before. Not unless they're following up something funny.'

'I haven't got anything infectious,' I assured her. 'He's probably someone I know from the hospital.'

'So you do have something wrong with you,' she said, folding her arms across her chest protectively. She didn't actually step backwards, but she did lean back.

'I used to work there,' I explained. 'I'm a doctor.'

If I'd told her that I had the plague I couldn't have produced a bigger reaction.

'You're a doctor!'

'Yes.'

'A proper doctor?'

'Yes.'

'You're very young.'

'I only qualified a year ago.'

'My oh my. Fancy me having a doctor staying here,' said the landlady. She seemed pleased. She had lowered her voice now that she knew I was a doctor. I got the impression that she didn't have many medical residents. Now that the threat had disappeared she unfolded her arms. 'Our own doctor in the house,' she said. She smiled at me. She had awful teeth.

'I suppose I'd better ring Dr Taylor and see what he wants,' I said. 'Do you know where the nearest phone is?'

'There's a pay phone in the bar,' she said. 'But you can use the phone in the office. It's more private. More suitable for a professional gentleman.' She turned and led the way downstairs and into her cramped office. It was barely large enough to contain a desk, a chair and a bookcase. The desk was piled high with papers. A large ashtray was filled with cigarette butts. The room stank of tobacco smoke. The bookcase was crammed with cheap paperbacks, mostly romances by Barbara Cartland and Georgette Heyer. 'I'll close the door for you,' she said. 'You may have private medical things to talk about. I know how you doctors are about confidentiality.' She squeezed past me. 'Oh, be careful of the chair,' she warned me. 'It's a bit wobbly.'

When she'd gone I sat down. Although I did so gingerly the chair very nearly succeeded in throwing me onto the floor. One of the four wheels had fallen off. I looked for the missing wheel but it was nowhere to be seen. I pulled the telephone towards me and dialled the number I'd been given.

'I gave my name to the woman who eventually answered. 'I was asked to call Dr Taylor.'

'Is it an emergency?' demanded the woman.

'No,' I said. 'But...'

'He doesn't take non emergency calls after 11.30 am,' said the woman sharply.

'I got a message to ring him,' I repeated. 'I gave her my name again.'

The receptionist's voice lowered to little more than a whisper.

'Did you say 'Doctor'?'

'Yes.'

'Oh I'm so sorry, doctor. I misunderstood. I thought you were a patient. I'll tell the doctor you're on the line.'

A moment or two later a gruff Irish voice spoke. 'Taylor here. I'm a GP. Single-handed practice in the city centre. Thanks for calling. You got my message. Chap I know at the hospital gave me your name. He does some locums for me. Patterson. You know him?'

'Yes, he's a good friend of mine.'

'He does locums for me when he can fit them in. Problem is that my wife booked theatre tickets for tonight and forgot to tell me. He can't cover for me tonight. I'm a single-handed practice and unless I can find someone to do it I can't go.'

'Oh. I'm sorry.'

'Can you manage to cover for me? Short notice I know. Thirty five quid cash for the night. Six pm to 8 am. That'll give me the whole night off.'

I listened in horror and excitement. 'I don't know,' I said. 'I've not done any general practice.'

'Patterson says you're fully registered.'

'Yes. I am. But...'

'No problem then. You've done casualty shifts?'

'Of course.'

'Got a car?'

'Yes.'

'Telephone?'

'This is a hotel. There is a telephone.'

'Splendid. They're a pretty well-trained bunch, my lot. They don't tend to ring much. Usually just kids with earache. Usual sort of thing.'

'I haven't got an emergency bag,' I said. 'I only left the hospital a day or two ago.'

'No problem there. I've got a spare emergency bag which

Patterson uses. You'll find everything you're likely to need in it. Where are you staying?'

I told him.

'I'll drop the bag off in an hour with the cash. And I'll pick the bag up tomorrow morning. You don't have to do anything.'

'What about the phone?' I asked.

'Just give me your number again,' he told me. 'We've got this clever telephone switching thing. I don't understand it but I can switch my phone calls through to your number. Works brilliantly. The patients don't even know they're being transferred. All automatic. Amazing what they can do isn't it?'

I agreed that it was.

When I put the phone down I was soaking with sweat.

I had never been so terrified in my entire life. Looking after patients in hospital, where they all lie in neat rows, ready diagnosed, lain out in pyjamas and nighties, was, it seemed to me, an entirely different matter to dealing with patients on the hoof. In the hospital the doctor is in charge. But would things be the same in the patient's home? And would I be able to find their homes? I would, I decided, have to find a map.

I was worried that my landlady would object to Dr Taylor putting his phone calls through to the hotel telephone. I need not have been concerned. Mrs Potter couldn't have been more delighted if I'd told her that the Queen would be coming to stay.

'The phone in the bar doesn't take incoming calls,' she told me when I'd explained what I'd wanted to do. 'But you can use the hotel phone.'

When I asked her if there would be a charge she'd dismissed the idea out of hand, as though she found the very thought of allowing commerce to intrude on our newly built professional relationship quite unacceptable.

# CHAPTER 7

There was no telephone in my room and no bed in the hotel's office so Mrs Potter suggested that I spend my night on call in the hotel's tiny bar.

'There's a comfortable chair in there,' she said. 'And you'll be able to hear the phone.'

And so, at six o'clock that evening, I sat myself down in the hotel bar for my first night's work as a general practitioner. I had my stethoscope in one jacket pocket and my car keys in the other. Beside me, on the floor, was Dr Taylor's spare medical bag. The battered, leather bag was filled with forms I didn't understand (including, I noticed to my horror, a book of death certificates and a book of forms with which I could apparently certify people insane), packets of drug samples and bits and pieces of elderly medical equipment. There was a portable sphygmomanometer in a black plastic box, an auriscope in a neat silver, metal box, an ophthalmoscope in a rather larger blue metal box, a patella hammer, a tape measure, a small torch, a pair of tweezers, a set of suture needles, a lancet with a packet of disposable blades, a Swiss Army penknife and, rather incongruously, a pair of pliers. There was a packet of the sort of thin pieces of wood which gardeners use to stick in the pots containing their cuttings. I hoped I wouldn't have to use the pliers. The bag was locked and the key was in my pocket with my car keys. A long white envelope containing my first wage packet as a proper doctor was nestling in my inside pocket. I hadn't opened it but it had crinkled reassuringly when I'd stuffed it into my pocket. Dr Taylor was paying me more for one night as his stand-in locum as I'd been paid for a fortnight as a hospital doctor.

Mrs Potter had warned me that there might be one or two calls from customers wanting to book rooms.

'Just tell them to ring again in the morning,' she had said. 'Tell them you're a doctor and that they're tying up a medical line.'

When I had asked her if she was worried at the prospect of losing potential customers she had simply shrugged. 'No one answers the phone at night,' she'd pointed out. 'We used to have an answering machine but I could never understand the messages people left so I gave it to my niece. She runs a little hairdressing business in Erdington.' She'd paused. 'At least that's what she says it is,' she'd added in a confidential whisper. 'Myself, I have my doubts. She has too many foreign holidays for a girl who just snips and perms for a living.' I didn't ask what business she thought her niece might be involved in, though it wasn't difficult to guess.

The phone didn't ring until half past ten. I had by then drunk three cups of coffee and four glasses of watered down lemonade. The caller was a young mother who was worried about her eighteen-month young son. 'Give me your address,' I told her briskly and, I hoped, reassuringly. 'I'll be there as soon as I can.'

'That's not Dr Taylor is it?'

I explained that I was standing in for him. She didn't seem to mind too much. 'I really just wanted a bit of reassurance, doctor,' she said. But I wasn't about to risk missing a case of meningitis or some other potentially deadly childhood ailment. I insisted that she gave me her address.

As luck would have it my newly acquired A to Z map showed that the address was no more than a mile from the hotel. I was there within minutes. It was a flat on the third floor of a poorly lit tower block. The lift didn't work and the stairwell had a nasty smell which suggested that there was probably a shortage of public conveniences in the area. I left the car on the main road two hundred yards away and hoped no one ran into it or stole it. It looked the sort of area where car radios didn't stay in the same vehicle for long. I knocked on the door with my knuckles. There was no doorbell and no knocker.

'Who's that?' demanded an angry male voice when I rang the doorbell. A television set was on. It sounded like some sort of game show. I'd been so busy working in hospital for a year that I'd hardly watched any television. I had no idea what programmes were showing.

'It's the doctor,' I called back.

'What the hell do you want?'

'Er, I was called to see a sick child,' I shouted back, rather hesitantly. This wasn't quite how I'd expected to be received. I had envisioned a pale, swooning mother standing on the doorstep with a flushed child in her arms.

'Stella, did you call the bloody doctor?' I heard the male voice shout.

'He's been bad all day,' a female voice shouted back at him. 'He's been crying.'

'There's bugger all wrong with him,' shouted the man who, even through a thin front door, sounded drunk.

'How would you know?' I heard the woman demand. 'You're never here.'

'I've been working,' shouted the man.

'You've been in the pub,' shouted the woman. 'You're pissed.'

Timidly, I knocked again. Almost immediately the door swung open. From the voice and manner I had expected the man who opened it to be at least six foot tall and fifteen stone. But he was nearly a foot shorter than I had thought, and five stones lighter. He looked to be in his forties.

'Don't be so bloody impatient,' he snarled.

'I'm sorry,' I said. 'But I have other patients to look after.' For the first time it occurred to me that in coming out I had left the phone unattended. I started to panic. Amazingly, everything had happened so quickly that I had never thought of this potential problem before.

'Are you giving it to my missus?' demanded the man.

I stared at him, bewildered and slightly shocked. 'I'm the doctor,' I repeated, rather stupidly. 'I was told you had a sick child.'

'Are you doing my missus?' the man repeated (though that was not quite the word he used).

'No,' I told him emphatically. 'I don't even know her. I've never been here before. I'm the doctor.'

'I know you're the doctor,' snarled the man. 'You keep telling me that. But doctors do it don't they? She's a good looking woman isn't she?'

'Well, I, er...' I stuttered.

'Get to bed you prat,' said a feminine voice, pushing the man aside. The owner of the voice was about half the age of her husband. And much bigger. She was taller, wider and considerably heavier. Muttering something I didn't hear, and probably wouldn't have wanted to, the man did as he was told.

'He's drunk,' she told me. It wasn't an apology. Just an explanation. 'The kiddie is in here.' She led the way into a tiny living room, lit only by a flickering television set and an electric fire. All three bars of the fire were lit. A small child was lying on the sofa covered with blankets.

I knelt by the side of the sofa, lifted off the blankets, and started to examine the boy who was asleep. He seemed hot but in addition to the blankets he was wearing three sweaters and the room was like a sauna. I took out my stethoscope and tried to listen to his chest. After a moment I gave up and turned to his mother who was now settled down again in front of the television set. 'I'm sorry,' I said, removing the earpieces of my stethoscope. 'But would you mind turning the television down a little?'

The woman turned the sound down a fraction, but didn't turn the television off as I had hoped she would. I listened to the boy's chest again. It sounded fine. As I finished he woke up and rubbed at his eyes with his fists. I examined his head and neck and checked his body for a rash. I looked in his ears, examined his eyes and used the torch to help me peer down his throat. Looking in the bag for something to hold his tongue down I realised that the thin wooden sticks were not intended for use in the garden but were, in fact, medical tongue depressors. We hadn't had them in hospital.

'His right ear looks a little inflamed,' I said, in the end.

The mother, still watching the television, half looked in my direction.

'I'll give you a course of antibiotics for him,' I said. I rummaged around in the bag, found several sachets of antibiotic medicine suitable for a child and gave them to her. 'Give him one of these every six hours. There's enough here for forty eight hours but you'll need to take him to the surgery tomorrow to get a prescription for the rest of the course.'

'Will he be all right, doctor?' she asked, showing some slight concern for the first time since I'd arrived.

'I'm sure he will,' I told her, with as much professional reassurance as I could muster. She didn't get up. But she smiled. She looked as though a weight had, temporarily at least, been lifted from her. I let myself out. I could hear her husband snoring.

★★★

As I walked back to my car I remembered a conversation I once had with Henry.

'That consultant cardiologist I see is a menace,' said Henry.

'He's supposed to be very good,' I said, rather defensively. 'He's written a textbook on heart abnormalities and loads of scientific papers on the subject.'

'He may well know his stuff,' agreed Henry. 'I'm not denying that. But the man is a menace. He may be clever with his books and his paperwork but he's no healer. I was waiting outside his office this morning and everyone I saw was terrified of him. The patients fear him – and so do the nurses. He's cruel and thoughtless.'

I didn't say anything. I'd seen the cardiologist in action. Indeed, I'd been on the receiving end of his 'wit and wisdom' myself on more than one occasion.

'A man and his wife came out of his office in tears,' said Henry. 'If I hadn't been in this damned chair I'd have gone in and flattened him.'

'Maybe they'd just been given bad news,' I suggested.

Henry shook his head. 'I talked to them while I waited to go in,' he said. 'The man had been told he had to lose two stones. He'd lost one and a half stones. Instead of congratulating him on the weight loss and encouraging him to carry on the cardiologist just asked him why he didn't just slit his wrists if he wanted to commit suicide.'

I felt embarrassed and said nothing.

'Someone should explain to him that people are frightened of doctors,' said Henry.

I looked at him. It wasn't something that had occurred to me before.

'Fear makes illness worse,' said Henry. 'So the doctor who calms his patients and puts them at ease will always be a better doctor.'

I remembered what he had said.

And I knew I would never forget it.

★★★

My car was still where I'd left it but someone had forced the passenger side window down and had stolen the radio. And either they or someone else had taken the hubcaps.

★★★

'Did the telephone go while I was out?' I asked the barman when I got back. The few customers who had been in the bar drinking had all disappeared. The barman, an elderly, weary looking man who was, so he told anyone who would listen, too old to be doing what he was doing, was tidying up, locking away the bottles of spirits and washing up dirty glasses in a small metal sink. His few strands of remaining hair were dyed black and combed over too much bald head. He wore a black blazer, blue trousers and a white shirt decorated with a clip on bow-tie.

'Not once,' he told me. 'I'm glad you're back. I'm going off now.'

I was glad to see him go. He was the most depressing person I'd ever met. After five minutes in his company I felt like drinking myself into a stupor. Perhaps that was why Mrs Potter employed him. I said goodnight, turned most of the lights off and settled down in the comfortable, battered old leather chair that Mrs Potter had recommended. I hadn't expected to go to sleep but I must have dropped off. And I hadn't yet acquired the doctor's ability to awaken immediately and fully upon hearing a telephone ring.

'This isn't the doctor's surgery,' I vaguely heard someone say as I blundered slowly back towards consciousness. 'You must have got the wrong number.' This seemed important but for a second or two I couldn't work out why.

Suddenly, I remembered where I was and why the call was important to me. I jumped up out of the chair as quickly as if someone had set fire to it and headed for the office. 'Don't put the phone down!' I called out just before I fell full length on the thin carpet. I had been lying awkwardly and although the rest of me was awake my left leg was still asleep.

'What's the matter?' someone asked. It was a feminine voice; the voice of a girl with a strong midland accent.

I looked up from the carpet. For a moment all I could see was a very long pair of legs. Slowly, I lifted my head to see what was above them. The girl who had spoken was about twenty years old; she was tall and slim and had long, dark brown hair. She was wearing patent leather shoes with five inch stiletto heels, black stockings with a patterned seam up the back, a black skirt shorter than the average pelmet (so short indeed that from my position on the floor I could tell that it was stockings and not tights that she was wearing) and a skimpy, black top with a scooped front and no sleeves. I vaguely recognised her from somewhere but couldn't think who she was or where I'd seen her before. She was carrying a very tiny black handbag. 'Don't put the telephone down, please,' I said. 'It's for me.'

'They want a doctor,' said the girl.

'That's me,' I said.

'You're the doctor?' said the girl, incredulously. She pointed at me and tried, unsuccessfully, to stifle a laugh. She pulled back the hand she'd used to point and put it over her mouth to hide her mirth.

'My leg gave way,' I explained. 'Cramp. Is there someone still on the phone?'

'It's a woman. She just says she wants a doctor. She didn't say why.'

I staggered to my feet, and stumbled into the hotel office. The telephone receiver was lying on the desk. I picked it up.

'This is the doctor,' I said. 'I'm standing in for Dr Taylor.'

'I need a call out,' said a gruff-voiced woman. She sounded very bad tempered.

'Can you tell me what's the matter?'

'I need a doctor.' The woman started coughing. I waited for her to stop and decided to abandon trying to find out what was wrong.

'What's your address?'

She told me.

'I'll be there as soon as I can,' I told her. I put the telephone receiver back on its cradle.

'So, you are a doctor.'

I turned round. The girl in the mini skirt was standing behind me. She had her arms folded across her chest. 'You're very young to be a doctor,' she said. I squeezed past her and went back into the bar. She leant back out of the way but not far enough to prevent me brushing against her. My A to Z map was in Dr Taylor's black bag. I took out the map and looked up Prospero Lane, the address the woman had given me. I couldn't find it listed in the index.

'Why are you running a doctor's surgery from a hotel?' asked the girl.

'A GP in town asked me to look after his patients for the night,' I explained.

'Is he paying you?'

'Yes. But I've got a problem. I can't find Prospero Lane on the map.'

'Is that where you've got to go?'

I nodded.

The girl screwed up her nose and closed her eyes for a moment. I waited. 'I think it's off the Wolverhampton Road,' she said at last. 'I'm pretty sure it is. My aunt Agnes lives down there. It's first left just past the Tivoli cinema on the dual carriageway.'

'The Tivoli cinema?'

'You couldn't miss it. It had a huge red sign. It's the one they

knocked down a couple of years ago. I think it's a car park now.'
She thought for a moment. 'Or is it the new council offices?'

I swore quietly and looked at my watch. It was twenty past three
in the morning. The night was not going well and I still had nearly
five hours to go.

'Is everything all right?'

We both turned at the sound of a new voice. It was Mrs Potter.
She was wearing a pink candlewick dressing gown. A matching pink
cord was tied firmly around her waist. She had about three dozen
pink and blue curlers in her hair.

'I heard voices,' she explained.

'I'm sorry,' I said.

'That's all right,' said Mrs Potter, waving a hand. 'I'm a very
light sleeper.'

'The doctor has had an emergency call,' explained the girl. She
lowered her voice as though this was secret information.

'Oh dear,' said Mrs Potter, sympathetically. 'Do you want me
to call an ambulance?' She reached for the telephone.

'No, no,' I said, holding up a hand to stop. 'I've got to go and
see what the problem is. But the address the patient gave me isn't
on the map.'

'It's Prospero Lane,' said the girl in the pelmet. 'It's just after the
Tivoli isn't it?'

Mrs Potter thought for a moment. 'Second left after the Tivoli,'
she agreed. 'Which end do you want?'

I looked at the piece of paper on which I had written the caller's
details. 'It's number 117b,' I said.

'I think that'll be the far end,' said Mrs Potter, with a nod of
certainty. 'Probably one of the flats.' She wrinkled up her nose. 'It's
a bit rough down there,' she said.

'Have you got a car?' asked the girl.

I nodded.

'Do you want me to take you there?'

'That would be very kind of you. I don't think I'll be able to
find it by myself. There won't be anyone wandering about to ask
at this time of night.'

'Or should I wait here and answer the phone?' asked the girl. 'What about if someone else calls?'

I bent down and picked up my black bag. I was faced with a real dilemma. If the girl didn't come with me I would probably never find Prospero Lane and the woman who had called would doubtless be found dead in her bed when someone missed her. If the girl did come with me the next caller, desperately searching for a doctor to treat her feverish child, would be left without medical help and her child would die.

If worrying was an Olympic sport I would, even at that young age, have been a serious contender for most of the main events. I could have worried well in the sprints (short, sudden worries about new problems) and I would have been just as successful in the marathon (masses of long-term, chronic never-ending worries). It now seemed to me that whatever I did there would be a disaster. And I would be responsible. My career as a doctor would be over before it had really started. What else could I do for a living once I had been struck off and publicly disgraced? I'd be lucky to get a job stacking shelves in the seediest of supermarkets. Once a committed worrier starts worrying there is no knowing where it will stop.

'Are you sure?' I heard the girl say.

'Of course I am, love,' said Mrs Potter. 'You go off and take the doctor to Prospero Lane. I'll hold the fort here. You just make sure you bring him back safe and sound.'

I looked at the girl and then at Mrs Potter.

'While you were daydreaming we sorted it,' explained the girl. 'I'll take you to Prospero Lane and Mrs Potter will answer the phone while you're out.'

We headed for the door, the car and the open road.

'I'll make a pot of tea,' said Mrs Potter as we left. 'It'll be nicely stewed by the time you get back.'

★★★

'I know this sounds corny,' I said. 'And I don't mean it to be. But haven't I seen you somewhere before?'

'At breakfast.'

I thought back. I couldn't remember her. 'There was a girl

who came in just as I was leaving,' I remembered. 'But she was blonde.'

'That was me,' said the girl.

I looked at her.

'Why did you dye your hair?'

She laughed. 'I haven't. It was a wig.'

'The blonde hair?'

'And this is a wig too.'

'Oh.' I said. I wondered what her hair was like underneath. 'Had you been out somewhere?' I asked, as I drove away from the hotel.

'I'm a dancer,' replied the girl. 'I work in a club in the centre of town.'

'I've never met anyone in show business before,' I said, impressed. I tapped at the wheel impatiently as I waited for the traffic lights in front of me to change from red to green.

'I've never met a doctor before,' she laughed. 'At least, not when I've had all my clothes on.'

'What's your name?'

The lights changed. I accelerated away from them.

'My work name is Tiffany. But my real name's Sarah.'

'Why do you work as Tiffany? Sarah's a lovely name.'

'Robert already had signs up advertising Tiffany. But the other Tiffany left. It was easier for me to change my name than for him to change the signs. What's your name?'

I told her. 'Who's Robert?' I asked. I speeded up so that we could get through the traffic lights ahead of us before they turned red.

'He's the boss,' she said. 'He owns the club. He's also my boyfriend.'

'How long have you been dancing for a living?'

'Six months. I was a dental nurse before that. But it was very dull. I hated it. And the dentist kept groping me between the patients.' She laughed. 'The customers try and grope me at the club but there's more room to get away from them. And the club has a strict no touch policy. Except for private arrangements, of course. The dentist was always catching me. My bum was black and blue every night. He was a pincher. And the money was terrible.'

'What sort of dancing do you do?' I asked.

'Oh, just move about and jiggle my bits,' she said. 'And I serve drinks too. But the serving drinks is just temporary. I need the job to get my Equity card and then I can get proper dancing jobs in theatres and on television. This is just a stepping stone really. A friend of mine says she thinks she can get us both jobs on a cruise liner. They do proper musicals on the ships and always need loads of dancers.'

'It all sounds very exciting,' I said. I stopped for another set of lights.

'Why don't you just go through?' asked the girl. 'There's nothing coming. And if the police pop out of the woodwork you've got a good excuse.' It made sense. I crept over the junction, looking carefully to the right and to the left.

'What about you?' she asked. 'How long have you been a GP?'

'Well, actually, this is my first night as a GP,' I confessed. 'I've just finished my pre-registration house jobs.'

'What does that mean?' she asked. 'Aren't you a proper doctor then?'

'Oh yes,' I said. 'When you qualify as a doctor you have to work for a year in hospital before you can be fully registered as a doctor.'

'What does that mean? Being registered?'

'It means that I can sign prescriptions and death certificates and things like that. And it means I can work outside the hospital. In the year after I qualified I could only work in a hospital as a junior doctor.'

'So now you're properly qualified?'

'Yes. I just haven't got a job yet.'

Just then a police car came swooping past us. The siren was sounding the blue light on the roof was flashing.

'Oh bugger,' I muttered. 'Was I speeding?' The police car cut in front of us and slowed. I slowed down too.

'I think so,' said Sarah. 'You were doing over fifty when I last looked.'

'What's the limit along here?'

'I think it's thirty.'

We both stopped. The near side door of the police car opened and a policeman got out.

'Tell him you're a doctor on your way to an emergency,' whispered Sarah. 'Maybe he'll let you off.'

The policeman walked over to my door. I wound down my window.

'In a hurry, were we sir?' he asked.

'Yes, I'm afraid so officer,' I said. 'I'm a doctor. On my way to an emergency.'

The policeman bent down and looked first at me and then at Sarah. 'Doctor? Emergency? Looks more like you're on your way to a party.'

'No, honestly,' I said. 'I'm a locum GP. My drug bag is in the boot.'

'Let's see it then,' said the policeman. He backed away from the door so that I could get out.

I got out, walked round to the boot and lifted Dr Taylor's black bag out. I unlocked it and showed the policeman the instruments and the drugs it contained.

'Where's the patient?'

I told him.

The policeman said nothing but walked back towards his car. He bent down and spoke to his colleague and then came back. 'We'll give you an escort, doctor,' he said. 'Follow us.'

And so we drove the rest of the way to Prospero Road behind a police car. The driver kept his siren and flashing lights switched on all the way. When we got to number 117b he skidded to a halt outside. I stopped a few feet behind him. 'Will you wait here?' I asked Sarah. 'Of course I will,' she replied. 'I'm not walking all the way back to the hotel.' I leapt out of the car, waved and shouted thanks, grabbed my black bag and dashed across a patch of bare grass to the front door. There was a small wooden sign explaining that no 117b was a first floor flat. I ran up the stairs and rang the bell.

'Are you the doctor?' asked the woman who answered the door.

She was in her mid sixties and grossly obese. She had varicose veins, swollen ankles and was wheezing.

When I said I was she turned and headed down a short narrow corridor. I followed her. Her feet were too big for her slippers and to get them on she had just crushed the backs of them with her heels. She headed into what was obviously her living room and sat down in an overstuffed easy chair. The room was full of teddy bears. There must have been a hundred of them.

'What's the problem?' I asked.

'I can't sleep,' said the woman. 'Dr Taylor gives me sleeping tablets but I ran out yesterday.'

I looked at her, disbelieving.

'I've forgotten the name,' she said. 'But I expect you'll know what they are. Dr Taylor will have told you. Blue and white they are.'

I said nothing but opened the black bag and rummaged around inside. I found three different types of painkiller, four different types of antibiotic, some antihistamines and numerous other pharmaceutical goodies. But no sleeping tablets. At last I found a bottle containing huge green and yellow capsules which I thought would do the trick.

'I haven't got any of the usual medicine you take,' I said. 'But I've got a bottle of very powerful sleeping capsules.' I picked out the bottle and examined it, hiding the label with my hand. 'The trouble is,' I told her, 'that these are very strong. Much stronger than the tablets you usually take.'

'Oh that's fine, doctor,' said the woman. 'Marvellous. I need something to knock me out.'

I hesitated. 'Are you sure you'll be all right with these?' I asked.

'Positive,' replied the woman. She held out a hand. 'Should I take it with water?'

'Definitely,' I told her. 'Lots of water.' I opened the bottle and shook one of the capsules out into her hand. 'Make sure you're in bed when you take it,' I warned her. 'You'll be asleep in minutes.'

'Thank you, doctor,' said the woman gratefully.

I closed and locked the black bag and headed for the door. When

I got back to the car Sarah was standing on the pavement talking to the two policemen. They saw me approaching, both waved and headed back to their car. 'Just thought we'd keep an eye on your nurse, doctor,' shouted one of the policemen.

'Was she OK?' asked Sarah, as we drove back into town.

'She wanted a sleeping tablet,' I said. 'She couldn't sleep.'

Sarah looked at me, clearly not sure whether or not I was kidding.

I drove back into town at 29 miles an hour and carefully stopped at every road junction, every pedestrian crossing and every set of traffic lights.

★★★

The three of us had been staring at the telephone for twenty minutes. Mrs Potter was sitting. Sarah and I were standing. We'd had an early breakfast.

When, at last, the phone rang I looked at my watch. It was three minutes past eight.

'Is that the doctor?' asked a female voice.

I said it was.

'This is Dr Taylor's receptionist,' said the voice. 'I'm taking the phones back now. Did you have a quiet night?'

'Oh yes,' I said. 'No problems.'

'Jolly good.' The phone clicked. I put the receiver back and leant back with a sigh.

'Are we off duty now?' asked Sarah.

I nodded.

'Phew,' said Mrs Potter, fanning her face with her hand. 'I'm exhausted.'

I reached into my inner jacket pocket and took out the envelope Dr Taylor had left me. I opened it. There were three ten pound notes and one five pound note. I handed one of the ten pound notes to the girl and one to Mrs Potter.

'What's this for?' demanded Sarah.

'Your help,' I said. 'I would have never have got through the night without you two.

'Are you sure?' asked Mrs Potter.

'Positive,' I said. The fiver I had left would pay for my petrol. And the remaining tenner would pay for half of a car radio if I bought a cheap, second-hand one. I could manage without hub caps. The night's work would have cost me ten pounds and four hub caps.

'I can't take this,' said the girl, holding the money out to me.

'Please,' I said.

With a sigh, Sarah folded the note and put it into her handbag. Mrs Potter slipped her ten pound note into her dressing gown pocket without protest.

'This makes us almost doctors,' giggled the girl to Mrs Potter.'

'Very respectable,' agreed Mrs Potter.

The phone rang. All three of us jumped. I reached out and answered it.

'I'd like a room for two for Saturday night,' said a male voice. 'Something with a view.'

'It's for you,' I said, handing the phone to Mrs Potter. She took it and reached for her booking diary and a pen.

'I think I'll go to bed,' I whispered, getting up and heading for the door.

'Me too,' said Sarah. I'm knackered.'

We headed up the stairs together.

'Thanks for all your help,' I said as we arrived at my door.

'I'm on the floor above,' said Sarah, pointing upwards. 'It was a pleasure.' She grinned and paused. 'I liked the police escort best,' she admitted. 'That was fun.'

'I expect I'll see you later on,' I said.

'Bound to,' said Sarah. She gave a little wave and scampered off up the stairs, her high heels click-clacking noisily on the varnished staircase. The stair carpet ended on the first floor. It was that sort of hotel.

★★★

I had finished my breakfast and was sitting staring at the pawn ticket I'd found among Henry's belongings.

'I've heard of people reading the cornflake packet or the sauce bottle at breakfast,' said Sarah, from behind me. 'But I've never seen anyone read a bus ticket before.'

'It isn't a bus ticket,' I told her. 'It's a pawn ticket.'

'Can I join you?' Sarah asked. Without waiting for an answer she sat down. 'A pawn ticket? Really? I didn't know pawn shops still existed. I thought they went out with Dickens.'

'There's a pawn shop just up the road,' I told her. 'That's where this is from.'

'Can I look?'

I handed her the ticket.

'What's it for?' she asked. Sarah, I had learned, had a child's innocence when it came to asking questions. She was not restrained by convention or modesty.

The young waitress came at that moment and took her breakfast order. I asked for more coffee and more toast.

'I don't know,' I told her, when the waitress had disappeared.

'How can you not know what your pawn ticket is for?'

'It's not mine.'

And then, without thinking about it and without really meaning to, I told her everything about Henry and Daphne. I told her how we'd met and I told her how much I loved the old couple and I told her that they had left the hospital when Henry had learned that Daphne was going to be put into a care home and would not be able to visit him.

'They ran away together?'

'Yes.'

'Like a young couple eloping?'

I laughed. 'Yes.'

'How absolutely romantic.'

'I suppose it is,' I admitted.

'And you think the pawn ticket could be a clue?'

'It could be,' I said. 'I haven't got much to go on. I'm wandering about in the dark.'

The waitress turned up with two racks of toast and two fresh pots of coffee.

'It's like a detective story,' said Sarah. 'I do love mysteries and adventures. Can I help?'

'You can,' I told her. 'But I don't know what to do next.'

'Well obviously the next thing to do is to find out what the pawn ticket is for!'

'I can't,' I told her.

'Why not?'

'It'll cost £60.'

'Crumbs. What is it? A gold watch?'

'I haven't got the faintest idea what it is. But I suspect that Henry must have pawned it to raise money for their getaway. He must have sent Daphne to the pawn shop.'

'I can lend you £60,' said Sarah.

'No!' I said firmly. 'You can't.'

'Yes I can. I've got £90. I save most of my tips. I'm saving up for a boob job.' She looked down at her breasts. 'If I'm ever going to get anywhere in show business I need bigger breasts.'

'I can't let you do that,' I said.

'Why not?' she demanded indignantly. 'You hardly know me. Besides they're my breasts.'

'No, I mean I can't let you find the money for the pawnbroker.'

'It's just a loan,' said Sarah, grabbing a slice of toast and covering it with about a quarter of an inch of butter. 'If the pawnshop lent Harry and Daphne £60 on it – whatever it is – then it must be worth more than £60 mustn't it?'

'Yes,' I agreed.

'So I'm not risking anything am I?' She put a piece of toast into her mouth and bit off a large chunk.

I buttered some toast and poured some coffee into my cup. 'It would just be a loan,' I insisted. 'I'll pay you back as soon as I can.'

'Good,' said Sarah, through a mouthful of toast. 'As soon as we've finished breakfast I'll go to the bank and then we'll go to the pawnshop.'

★★★

'There's a call for you, doctor,' said Mrs Potter as I left the breakfast room, brushing toast crumbs from my jacket. She handed me a piece of paper with a number written on it. 'I think it's that doctor's surgery again,' she told me. 'They're probably so pleased with your work the other night that they want to hire you again.'

I rang the number and spoke to Dr Taylor.

'Patient of mine in Prospero Lane,' he said. 'A Mrs Wilkins. Do you remember seeing her last night?'

I remembered immediately. How could I ever forget Prospero Lane. I felt cold inside. What had I done wrong? Had I killed her. Would I be hauled before the General Medical Council and struck off? Or maybe taken to court and charged with murder?

'She likes your sleeping tablets better than the ones I used to give her,' said Dr Taylor. 'Swears she slept twice as well as she'd ever slept before.'

'Oh good,' I said, relief flooding through my mind.

'So, what were they?' he asked.

'I gave her a big green and yellow vitamin capsule I found in your bag,' I told him. 'I couldn't find the sleeping tablets.'

'Splendid,' said Dr Taylor. 'I'll prescribe some of those for her. Thanks doctor. I'll ring you again when I need cover if I may.'

'Yes, certainly,' I said, though I would, I thought, have to renegotiate the financial arrangements.

He put the phone down and so did I.

# CHAPTER 8

'This is quite exciting,' said Sarah.

'Because we don't know what it is?'

'It could be anything!'

'Well, I think it's a fair guess that it isn't an elephant or a fruit farm.'

'You know what I mean,' laughed Sarah. 'What do you think it is?'

'I think it's probably jewellery,' I said.

'I thought that,' agreed Sarah. 'A watch.'

'Maybe,' I agreed.

'Perhaps he had a gold watch which he inherited or which he was given when he retired.'

'Possibly.' I was hoping that whatever it was it would give us a clue to where Henry and Daphne had gone. An address would be wonderful. A clue would be useful.

We arrived at the door to the pawnbroker's and went in. I put Henry's ticket through the grille at the hatchway. The man I'd spoken to on my previous visit wasn't there. He had been replaced by a woman in her sixties. She had short, white hair and the wrinkled eyes of a long-term smoker. She checked the ticket against the ledger. I handed her a big chunk of Sarah's savings. She gave me a stout brown envelope sealed with a metal clip. The envelope had a number written on it which matched the number on the ticket I'd taken in. I took the envelope and thanked her. We left.

'Open it!' said Sarah, as soon as we were outside in the street.

'Not here,' I said. 'We need to go somewhere private. We'd better go back to the hotel.'

'I can't wait that long. Come in here!' Sarah dragged me into a coffee bar. Birmingham had quite a few of them in those days. The coffee bar was virtually empty. We found a booth in a dark corner. A waitress came. I ordered two coffees and resisted Sarah's demands that I open the envelope until the coffees had been delivered.

We both pushed our coffees away to one side of the table. I unfastened the metal clip which fastened the envelope, tilted the envelope and gently poured the contents out onto the table.

The envelope had contained a small red box. The box, made of leather, was about two inches square and well-worn. I picked it up and examined it. There was absolutely no clue on it as to what it might contain. There wasn't even a name of a shop or a maker.

'Open it!' whispered Sarah.

I opened it.

Neither of us had expected what we found. It wasn't a watch or a brooch. It wasn't a rare coin or a bracelet. It was a medal. A round medal with a piece of coloured ribbon attached to it.

'What is it?' asked Sarah, clearly as puzzled as I was.

'It's a medal.'

She looked at me.

'I don't know what sort of medal.' I said.

'But obviously quite a valuable medal.'

'Worth more than sixty quid anyway,' I agreed.

'Was Henry in the war?'

'He was in the First World War,' I told her. 'He was injured.'

'What happened?'

'A bullet shot his thumb off.'

'Which thumb?'

'I don't know.' I held up my hands and looked at them, trying to remember. 'The left one.'

'Would they give him a medal for losing a thumb?'

'I wouldn't have thought so,' I said.

'Nor would I,' said Sarah. 'If they gave people valuable medals for losing a thumb what would they hand out to people who lost legs?' She stopped and thought for a moment. 'I'm sorry,' she said. 'That sounded awful. It must have been awful to lose a thumb. But you know what I mean.'

I nodded and smiled at her. 'I know what you mean,' I agreed.

'Who will know what sort of medal this is?' asked Sarah.

'I noticed an antique shop four or five doors away,' I told her. 'He's got medals in the window.'

'Let's ask him,' said Sarah, sliding out of the booth.

'Hey!' shouted a voice as we left.

We both turned.

'You might not like the coffee,' said the waitress. 'But you've still got to pay for it.'

Red-faced I apologised, paid her for the coffee and gave her a big tip.

★★★

The antique shop had a CLOSED sign in the window. But I tried the door anyway. It was unlocked. I opened it and we went in. Inside I called out, rather timidly, asking if there was anyone there.

'Is anyone in?' yelled Sarah, without waiting to see if my tentative enquiry produced any results.

Moments later a small, thin, wiry man with a pair of jeweller's magnifying glasses perched on the end of his nose appeared. He was eating a ham roll and had mustard on his chin. He seemed about to tell me off for ignoring the closed sign but then he saw Sarah and his face lightened. She explained that we just wanted him to look at a medal for us.

'It's a George Medal,' he said. 'Issued during the Second World War.' He put down the roll and turned the medal over and over in his hand. 'This one is quite unusual,' he said. 'It was awarded to a soldier but the George Medal isn't usually a military medal. It's usually awarded to civilians.'

'So how did this come to be awarded to a soldier?'

The antique dealer shrugged. 'I have no idea. Maybe he did something exceptionally brave when he was off duty.' He thought for a moment. 'Perhaps he rescued a child from a burning house as he made his way home on leave. Who knows? All I can tell you is that it's only ever given after some act of great bravery.'

'And this was definitely for something that happened in the Second World War?'

'Oh yes, definitely.'

I remembered the newspaper cutting and the story about how Michael Mulligan had won a George Medal for rescuing people from a train crash.

'How much is the medal worth?' asked Sarah.

The dealer looked at the medal again. 'I would give you £200 in cash for it,' he said. 'But I could get considerably more if you leave it with me and let me find a buyer for you. It's a very special medal.'

'We'll have to think about it,' I said. 'It belongs to a friend.'

The dealer looked at me, frowning. 'Doesn't he know why he got the medal?' he asked.

'He's not well,' I said. 'He's quite old. You know how it is.'

'Ah, I know only too well,' replied the dealer. 'My wife...' He left the sentence unfinished.

We thanked him and headed for the door. He picked up his ham roll and carried on where he'd left off.

★★★

Something had been troubling me for hours. I should have pushed earlier. But I was so desperate to get the packet from the pawnbroker that I hadn't.

'Where did you get the money from?' I asked.

Sarah looked at me, as though she didn't understand what I meant.

'The money for the pawnbroker.'

'It was money I'd saved.' A pink flush appeared on her cheeks.

I said nothing but just looked at her. She slowly went a brighter and brighter red.

'Where did it come from Sarah?' I asked her. 'I just want to know.'

'I did a favour for Robert.'

'What sort of favour?'

'A German businessman came over. They're opening a club together in Hamburg.'

'What was the favour?'

'He wanted me to be nice to him.'

'How nice?'

'Just nice. It wasn't important.'

'And Robert gave you money?'

'No. It wasn't like that.'

I put my head in my hands and said nothing.

'I don't know what you're getting so upset about. It wasn't a big deal. If a bloke takes me out for a meal he expects me to sleep with him whether I'm in love with him or not. This way I didn't have to bother eating the soggy chicken and putting up with all sorts of bullshit about how much money he earned. And the money helped us get the medal from the pawnshop didn't it?'

'I thought Robert was supposed to be your boyfriend?'

'He is. I just did him a favour. It took less than an hour. How long does it take you to earn sixty quid?'

★★★

There was a bang on my door that night, just as I was about to go to sleep.

'I think I've got an infection,' said Sarah. She had come in without waiting to be told to do so.

I looked at her.

'It must have been that German.' She told me this with no sense of embarrassment or anger.

I still didn't say anything.

'Can you give me an antibiotic or something?'

'No.'

'I don't want to go to the doctor.'

'Why not?'

'You can give me a prescription.'

'I can't give you a prescription without examining you.'

She started to unfasten her blouse. 'That's OK. Examine me.'

'No!' I put a hand out to stop her. 'You need tests. You have to go to the doctor.'

'But you're a doctor.'

'Yes. But not your doctor. If you don't want to go to your GP just pop along to the hospital. They have clinics on Tuesday and Thursday evenings.'

She left, slamming the door behind her.

# CHAPTER 9

I woke up in the middle of the night suddenly realising that I did have a lead after all. From the newspaper cutting I knew the regiment in which Private Mulligan had served and all army regiments keep records. Maybe the record keeper at Private Mulligan's old regiment might be able to help me.

At seventeen minutes past nine the next morning I was on the telephone to the regiment's records office. It had taken me, and a very helpful operator from directory enquiries, that long to find the number. The man I was talking to had introduced himself as Captain Richmond.

'I'm sorry to bother you,' I said. 'But I'm a doctor calling from the Birmingham hospital and I'm hoping that you can help me with some information.'

'What sort of information?' asked Captain Richmond.

'A patient of mine has gone missing,' I explained. 'He's rather old and confused and tends to wander a bit. The problem is that his medical records don't show any addresses that he might have gone to. He needs medication rather urgently and so it's important that I find him as quickly as possible.' I crossed my fingers as I spoke and hoped that my good intentions would mean that Gabriel wouldn't hold the lie against me when he came to do the final summing up.

'What's his name?' asked Captain Richmond.

'Private Mulligan,' I told him. 'Private Michael Mulligan.'

'I don't suppose you have a number for him?'

'No, sorry.'

'What's your number? I'll ring you back. I should be able to get something for you in half an hour or so.'

I gave him the hotel number and then raced upstairs and banged on Sarah's door. 'Are you in?' I shouted.

'What's the matter?' she demanded. She was holding a lipstick in her left hand.

'I need you to answer the phone in half an hour's time,'

'Downstairs?'

I nodded.

'I'll be down in twenty minutes. Is that OK?'

'That's fine.'

I raced back downstairs to ask Mrs Potter if I could commandeer her telephone once more. 'It's in a good cause,' I assured her.

'Are you still trying to find that patient you lost?'

I said I was.

'If I ever get lost I hope my doctor puts as much effort into finding me,' she said.

★★★

Captain Richmond telephoned almost exactly thirty minutes after we had spoken. Sarah answered the phone. 'Birmingham Hospital,' she said, in her very poshest voice.

'I'll just see if he's available,' she said, when the officer asked to speak to me. 'But at this time of the morning the doctor is usually either in his clinic or the operating theatre.'

I tried to grab the phone off her but she put her hand over the receiver and held it out of my reach.

'Come on!' I hissed. 'Give me the phone.'

'Don't be in such a hurry,' said Sarah calmly. She waited another ten or fifteen seconds and then gave me the phone.

'Hello,' I said. I was out of breath with anxiety and hoped Captain Richmond would assume that it was because I had been running.

'Ah, doctor,' said the Captain. 'I've managed to track down your Private Mulligan. I've got a next of kin address for him but I'm not sure how up-to-date it is. Private Mulligan left the army in 1946.'

'It'll be a start anyway,' I said.

Captain Richmond gave me an address in Birmingham. It was no more than five miles away from Mrs Potter's hotel. 'I don't know who these people are,' he said. 'But we've got a Doris Dickson of that address down as next of kin.'

★★★

Mr and Mrs Dickson lived in a terraced house in what had once been a poor part of town but which had, in recent years, been subjected to what estate agents refer to as 'gentrification'. This meant that the traditional paving slabs had all been ripped up and replaced with bricks. The old-fashioned cast iron lampposts which had previously lit the street had been ripped out, sold for scrap and replaced by imitation old-fashioned lampposts made out of something lighter and probably far less durable. There were hanging baskets full of plastic flowers dangling from brackets attached to alternate houses.

I found number 56 and rang the doorbell. An old woman in a pinafore came to the door. She had grey hair, neatly permed, and underneath her pinafore she wore a dress with lots of flowers on it. I introduced myself. She confirmed that she was Mrs Dickson.

'Come in,' she said. She stepped back so I could squeeze past her. Like Mrs Dickson the hallway was welcoming but narrow but neat. There were hunting prints on the wall and at the far end of the hallway a grandfather clock was ticking loudly.

'First left,' called a male voice.

I took the first doorway on my left and found myself in a small, overcrowded room. There was a sofa, two armchairs and a table covered in an antimacassar. There were two glass-fronted bookcases in the room and both were crammed with books; most were old hardbacks which had long since lost their dustjackets. There were neat piles of magazines and newspapers in one corner of the room. A third glass-fronted cupboard was filled with glassware and china. There were numerous pictures on the walls, mostly old Victorian prints, and a few ornaments hanging on nails. There were even three plaster ducks flying up one wall. Both my grandmothers used to have plaster ducks on their walls.

An old man in a red cardigan and grey trousers was sitting in one of the armchairs. Beside him there was an open bookcase. Fixed to the arm of his chair there was a writing surface. He had a full head of grey hair, neatly combed, and large, bushy eyebrows which he also kept neatly combed. He wore tweed slippers. He had one leg crossed over the other and I noticed that the sole of one slipper had worn through. I could see the sole of a red sock.

'Mr Dickson?'

He nodded.

I introduced myself. 'I'm a doctor. I'm trying to trace Michael Mulligan,' I said to the old man. 'He was in the army during the war and the army records people have a Doris Dickson of this address down as his next of kin.'

The old man nodded. I could hear his wife talking to herself in the kitchen. 'Kettle. Water. Pot. Tea. Cups. Saucers.' She was telling herself what to do. 'Kettle. Water. Pot. Tea. Cups. Saucers.'

'She forgets things sometimes,' explained the old man. 'She gets flustered.'

'I understand,' I said.

'They say there isn't anything they can do for her.'

'No, I'm afraid there probably isn't.'

'You say you're a doctor?'

'I am.'

'Do you work at the hospital?'

'I used to. A Mr Henry Mulligan was a patient of mine. He's missing at the moment and I'm trying to find him. I'm trying to trace Michael Mulligan in the hope that he will be able to tell me where I can find Henry.'

'So how did you come to lose him?'

'He discharged himself. I think he's gone off with his wife. I think they're both in danger. I need to find them both quickly but I don't know where they've gone.'

'What sort of danger? Is someone after them?'

'No, no.' I shook my head. 'Not that sort of danger. Mr

Mulligan's health isn't very good. He really needs to be in hospital.' I said. I didn't see any point in telling the old man what my fear really was.

'I don't think I can help you,' said Mr Dickson.

'If you could give me any idea where I might find him, that would help a lot.'

The old man stared at me, as though trying to make a decision.

'You're not from the police?'

'Good heavens no!'

'You're definitely a doctor?'

'Yes.'

He reached up to the shelf beside him and pulled down a dictionary. He opened it and thumbed through the pages. 'Spell diarrhoea.'

'I beg your pardon?'

'Spell diarrhoea,' he repeated.

I spelt diarrhoea.

'Right,' he said. 'I don't expect a policeman would be able to spell diarrhoea.'

'Probably not,' I agreed.

'Do you doctors still take an oath to keep things confidential?' he asked me.

'We do,' I said. 'The Hippocratic Oath.'

He reached up to the shelf again and pulled down another book. He flicked through the pages, found what he was looking for. 'Here it is,' he said. 'Whatever in connection with my medical practice, or not in connection with it, I see or hear, in the life of men, which ought not to be spoken of abroad, I will not divulge, as reckoning that all such should be kept secret.'

'That's from the Hippocratic Oath,' I agreed.

'So, you're bound by that if I tell you something.'

'I am,' I agreed.

He stared at me, as though trying to see into my soul. 'Are you an honest man,' he asked.

'I think so,' I said. 'I do my best. My only interest in Henry Mulligan is that I want to help him. He's my friend.' And I explained to the old man how Henry and I had met.

'OK.' said the old man, with a big sigh. 'I'll tell you something I promised I'd never tell another soul.'

I waited.

'Michael Mulligan was never in the army.'

I thought about this for a moment. 'But the army have a Michael Mulligan on their records,' I pointed out. 'And I have a newspaper cutting with a photograph of Michael Mulligan receiving a medal.' I reached into my pocket and took out the cutting. I handed it to Mr Dickson.

'That's Michael Mulligan,' I told him.

'It is,' he said. 'But he was never in the army.'

I stared at him for a moment trying to take this in. 'The man in the picture was a soldier,' I said. 'He was in the army. He was given a medal.'

'Oh, it's Michael Mulligan,' said the old man. 'But he was no hero.'

'How do you know?' I asked. 'How can you be so sure?' I didn't understand.

'Michael Mulligan didn't serve in the army at all. He was a coward and a crook and he broke my daughter's heart.'

'Your daughter was Doris?'

He nodded. 'They were engaged.'

'During the war?'

'They got engaged in 1938. She was just seventeen. Pretty as a picture and innocent as a lamb.' He opened a drawer beside him and took out an old blue diary. He opened the diary and took out a photograph. He looked at the photograph for a moment and then handed it to me.

The picture was of a young girl. She was wearing a polka dot dress and a big straw hat. There was a beach and some sea behind her. I turned the photograph over. There was writing on the back. 'Doris, Westward Ho! 1937.'

'We went on holiday, the three of us, in 1937,' explained Mr Dickson. 'We went every summer. That's where Doris met Michael. She was bowled over by him.'

'Is Doris still...' I hesitated. Somehow I knew the answer and wished I hadn't asked the question.

'She died in 1957,' said Mr Dickson. 'They said it was cancer but it was heartbreak.' He paused and wiped away another tear. 'Michael Mulligan killed her,' he said.

'I'm sorry,' I told him.

He reached up an arthritic hand and wiped a tear away from the corner of an eye. 'She was a lovely girl,' he said. 'Never hurt anyone. She deserved better than Michael Mulligan.'

'What happened?'

'Michael was called up for the army but he didn't want to go. He was terrified. He wet himself the day he got his call-up papers.'

'But he did go,' I said. 'In the end he went.'

Mr Dickson shook his head. 'Michael didn't go,' he said. 'His uncle went for him.'

'His uncle?'

'Henry Mulligan,' said Mr Dickson.

I stared at him. I don't know what I'd expected to hear but this hadn't been it.

'Henry was Michael's uncle. You knew that?'

I shook my head. 'Henry never mentioned anyone called Michael.'

'I'm not surprised,' said Mr Dickson. 'He was probably too ashamed. He and Daphne did everything they could for that boy. They treated him like a son. Brought him up. Looked after him. Did everything a couple could. He treated them like dirt. The same as he treated everyone. He was bad news that boy.'

'But how could Henry pretend to be Michael?'

'They just swapped identities,' said Mr Dickson. 'There was only a few years between them and Henry always kept himself in good condition. He was a professional cyclist between the wars. Did you know that?'

I shook my head. It seemed that there was a lot about Henry that I didn't know.

'He took part in the Tour de France once. Maybe more than once. He rode for one of the British manufacturing teams. I can't remember which one. He was a mechanic and loved machines. He rode a bicycle at weekends and then entered a few races and won some of them. So he got put in for the Tour de France. No one over here had heard of it really. But it was big news in France and on the continent. He had a bad crash coming down a mountain and couldn't have children. That's why he and Daphne never had any kids of their own.'

'Henry told me once that he hadn't been able to be a proper husband to Daphne.'

Mr Dickson nodded. 'He maybe wasn't much of a husband in the bedroom but he was a good husband in every other way.'

For a few moments I didn't speak. I was still trying to absorb everything Mr Dickson had told me.

'So Henry pretended to be Michael Mulligan and took his place in the army?'

Mr Dickson nodded.

'Because Michael was too frightened to go?'

'Michael tried, and failed, to get out of the call-up. He got a bent doctor to say he wasn't fit. But the doctor got arrested for providing false certificates and Michael got called up. He was hysterical with fear.'

'And it was Henry, not Mulligan, who rescued those people in the train crash?'

'Of course. Michael wouldn't lift a finger to help anyone. He was the most cowardly man I ever knew. I think there was something missing in his make-up. He was a thoughtless, selfish bastard. Henry was something else. He was a real gentleman. He had an arm broken in the crash but he still kept going back into the wreckage rescuing people.'

'I didn't know he broke his arm,' I said. 'It didn't mention the arm in the newspaper.'

'I don't think Henry ever mentioned it,' said Mr Dickson. 'He never liked a fuss.'

'And where was Michael while Henry was pretending to be him?'

'Michael was away somewhere. In hiding,' said Mr Dickson. 'Before the war Henry and Daphne had a garage in Walsall. They were quite well off. It had started off as a bicycle repair shop. Then they did motorcycles and finally moved on to cars. Henry was a brilliant mechanic. When Henry went off to the war he told Daphne to sell the garage and to go to the country. Daphne was always delicate. Henry wanted her to be somewhere safe where he wouldn't have to worry about her. He knew she wouldn't be able to run the garage without him.'

'So Daphne sold the garage?'

'She sold it and Michael persuaded her to let him look after the proceeds.'

'A mistake?'

'Big mistake,' nodded Mr Dickson. 'Michael and Daphne moved to Devon and rented a cottage. Our Doris went with them. Michael got rid of all the money and to top it all he ended up in prison for fraud. He also found time to ditch our Doris. She had to hitchhike her way back home. He didn't even give her the money for the train.'

'But Henry couldn't serve the prison sentence for Michael? Henry was in the army.'

Mr Dickson nodded. 'But Michael served the sentence as Henry so it was Henry who got the criminal conviction in his name. Even if he'd wanted to Michael couldn't have told anyone his real name when he was arrested. He'd have been in even bigger trouble if he had.'

'Do you know what it was that Michael did?'

Mr Dickson shrugged. 'Some small time fraud. Petrol coupons I think it was. He and some other chap were printing them. He was a con man all his life. After the war, when he got the medal, he almost managed to get himself elected to Parliament. But people saw through him. You know what they say. You can fool some of the people.'

'And Daphne? What happened to her when Doris came back here?'

'Daphne couldn't afford the rent on the cottage because Michael had spent everything. She moved into a little chalet. It was out of season and they were very cheap to rent.'

'But it was Michael who collected the medal that Henry was awarded?'

'The medal wasn't handed out until after the war. By that time Henry was back to being Henry and Michael fancied himself as a war hero. The two men looked very similar. They looked more like brothers than father and son. It wasn't difficult.'

'But Henry wasn't Michael's real father?'

'No, no,' said Mr Dickson. 'Henry was Michael's uncle.'

The old man pointed a finger at the photograph. 'That's Michael,' he said. 'The man in the picture has a thumb on his left hand,' he said. He jabbed at the hand with which the soldier in the picture was holding up his medal. Four fingers and a thumb were clearly visible.

'And Henry, of course, had no thumb on his left hand.'

The old man nodded. He looked at me. 'Do you know how he lost it?'

'It was shot off during the First World War,' I replied.

The old man nodded. 'But he used to tell people he lost it in an industrial accident.' He sipped at his tea. 'He never got any compensation for it, you know.'

'I know,' I said.

'He fought in two wars, lost one thumb and had his medal stolen from him,' said Mr Dickson. 'Drink your tea,' he said. 'It'll go cold.'

'One more thing,' I said a little later. 'Do you know what happened to Michael in the end?'

'He died a few years ago. Heart attack I think it was. He was broke. He had no relatives except Henry and Daphne. They ended up paying for the funeral. One good thing, though, I think Henry got his medal back. It was among Michael's things.'

I stayed for a second cup of tea and a piece of ginger cake. Then I drove away. I felt sad. It was impossible to spend time in that house without feeling sad. The sorrow had seeped into the brickwork and the furniture.

I had learned a lot from Mr Dickson about Henry. But I was still no nearer to finding out where Henry had gone. At least, I didn't think I was. In fact, Mr Dickson had given me the answer I was looking for but I'd just been too stupid to realise it.

# CHAPTER 10

I was sitting on my bed trying to decide which of two dirty shirts was the cleanest when the door burst open and Sarah exploded into the room.

'I'm dying!' she announced. 'I've caught something awful.' She was wearing a thin, pink cotton nightdress which had a picture of a rabbit on the front.

I stood up and pulled on the shirt I was holding. 'What's the matter?' I asked, tucking the shirt into my trousers.

'I've got this terrible rash,' she told me. 'It's all over my body. Do you think I'll die?' She started to cry.

'Have you seen a doctor?' I asked her.

'I'm seeing a doctor!' she said angrily. 'I want you to tell me what's wrong. Just tell me if I'm going to die.'

'I'm not supposed to run surgeries in my bedroom,' I told her. 'Why not?'

I tried to think of a reason but couldn't. 'I'm not sure,' I muttered. 'But you're a friend and I'm not properly dressed yet.'

'We're not sleeping together,' Sarah pointed out.

'No,' I agreed. 'Did you go to the hospital?'

'Yes. But this has started since I went to the hospital. They said I had an infection and gave me some pills for it. But they must have missed something.'

'What symptoms have you got?'

She lifted up her nightdress. She was naked underneath it. Her breasts were even smaller than advertised. Her whole body was covered with a pink rash.

'You've got a rash,' I said, after a moment's observation.

'I know that,' she said, impatiently.

'Does it itch?'

'It's driving me mad,' she said. 'And how can I go to work like this? I look stupid!' She pulled her nightie right up to her chin and peered down at her chest. 'Some of these spots are bigger than my breasts!' she complained.

'What tablets are you taking?'

'I don't know.'

'Can you get them?'

'Now?'

'Yes.'

She allowed her nightie to fall back down and left. Less than a minute later she was back with a small brown bottle which she handed to me.

'They're white,' she said. 'Will you know what they are?'

I looked at the label. 'Probably not,' I admitted. 'But the name is on the bottle.' I handed the bottle back to her. 'You're taking penicillin and you've got a penicillin rash.'

'The tablets I'm taking caused this?'

'I'm afraid so.'

'What do I do now?'

'You'd better go back to the hospital and ask them whether they want you to stop the penicillin or to carry on with it.'

Sarah glowered at me and started to leave. 'I wouldn't mind sleeping with you,' she said, turning back from the door. 'If you want to. But we'd have to be very secretive about it because my boyfriend is very jealous.'

'This is Robert, the same boyfriend who persuaded you to sleep with the German businessman?'

'That was just a favour,' she said angrily. She flounced out and slammed the door. A moment later the door opened again.

'Your shirt needs ironing,' said Sarah. 'It's horribly creased.'

'It needs washing before it needs ironing,' I told her.

'Ask Mrs Potter,' said Sarah. 'If you smile nicely she'll let you borrow her washing machine and her iron.'

'Thank you,' I said.

'Don't mention it,' she replied.

And she left again.

★★★

I was heading out of the hotel on my way to try and find George Pardoe in Worcester when I met Sarah coming in. She was wearing jeans and a long-sleeved man's shirt. She also wore dark glasses and had a scarf wrapped around her neck. There was hardly an inch of skin visible.

'What did the hospital say about your rash?'

'They changed the tablets and gave me something else. They said the rash should go in a couple of days.'

'Are you going to work?'

'Don't be potty. I can't work like this. I look like a freak. The customers would all think I'd got leprosy or smallpox and they'd leave in droves.'

'I'm sorry.'

She shrugged. 'That's what happens when you do a favour for someone.' She looked down at the small bag I was holding.'

'Are you going out on a call?'

I shook my head.

'Where are you going then?'

'I've got a lead that might take me to Henry and Daphne. I'm driving to Worcester. I might have to stay the night.'

'Don't you dare move an inch!' said Sarah, pointing a finger at me. 'I'll be back in two minutes.'

'Why?' I called after her.

But she'd gone.

Ignoring her orders I walked to the car park and collected the car. I drove back and parked alongside the kerb outside the hotel. Less than a minute later Sarah appeared. She was struggling with a huge blue suitcase.

'What on earth have you got there?' I demanded.

She heaved the suitcase into the back of the car and climbed in beside me. She leant her head forward and peered at me over the top of her dark glasses. 'Just a few overnight things,' she explained. 'I'm coming with you,' she said.

It was a statement not a request.

I started the engine and we set off for Worcester.

★★★

George Pardoe no longer lived at the address I had for him. But the bright young couple who had bought the house from him knew where he'd gone. He was living in a old people's home overlooking the river. 'It's a very nice position,' said the woman, an emaciated creature whose most memorable features were very short pure white hair and enormous dangly earrings which almost reached her shoulders.

We arrived at the home at 8 pm. We were both starving hungry but I suspected that if we ate before going to the home Mr Pardoe might well have been put to bed and locked up for the night.

We needn't have worried. Mr Pardoe was playing poker with three other residents. They each had a bottle of beer in front of them and they appeared to be playing for money. They didn't look as if they were about to be put to bed.

When a woman in a blue uniform told Mr Pardoe he had visitors he finished his hand, whispered something to his companions and then walked over to where we were standing. He walked with a limp but held himself as straight as a guardsman.

I introduced myself and Sarah and told him we were looking for Henry Mulligan and wondered if he could help.

'What makes you think I can help?' he asked rather warily.

'Because your name and address appear in Henry's address book,' I told him. 'The only other person in there is a niece of Daphne Mulligan's. She lives in Australia. You were closer.' I smiled at him.

'May I ask what you were doing looking through Henry's address book?'

I explained, keeping the explanation as succinct as I could.

'You'd better come into the dining room,' said Mr Pardoe. 'It'll be empty. We can talk there.' He led us into a smart room which contained a dozen small tables and twice as many chairs. The tables had all been set, presumably for breakfast. There were real flowers on all the tables. Mr Pardoe sat down. Sarah sat next to him. I turned a third chair round and sat opposite him.

'I haven't seen Henry for a long time,' he said. 'But we raced together in France and we kept in touch.'

'You were a cyclist?' I remembered Mr Dickson had told me.

He nodded. 'We were among the first Britons to take part in the Tour de France,' he said. 'We neither of us ever completed it. The whole thing was a nightmare. The roads were rough and the bicycles we rode were crude and very heavy compared to today's machines.'

'It must have been quite an ordeal,' I said.

'The first time we went Henry fell badly. One of his front forks broke. Just snapped like a breadstick. He was thrown over the handlebars and landed on the road. We were descending a rough mountain track at the time. I was about a hundred yards in front of him but I heard the crash. I went back and found him yards from the edge of a 300-foot drop. He was unconscious. I had to wait for one of the support cars to arrive and they took him to a hospital in the next town. He broke two ribs and an arm and lost several teeth. He'd also crushed his...' he looked at Sarah. She nodded to encourage him to continue. 'He'd crushed everything against the crossbar when the fork had snapped. They had to remove both his testicles and do extensive repair work on all the rest of it. They weren't too good at that sort of thing. It was just a small town hospital. He never rode a bicycle again. But the next year he went back with me as my mechanic. He drove a Citroën van as the support vehicle. We were together in France when Henry got the news about his brother.'

'That would be Michael's father?'

'That's right. Though the father was called Michael too so it gets a bit confusing.'

'What was the news Henry received?'

'He got a telegram to say that his brother was dead. It hit him hard. They weren't close in the way that some brothers are. They weren't always in each other's pockets if you know what I mean.' He looked at me. I nodded to show that I understood what he meant. 'But they were close emotionally. They'd have done anything for one another. Michael was quite a bit older than Henry but they were as close as any two brothers I've ever known.'

'Henry got a train to Paris and then took the train to Calais and London. He was worried about me but I told him to go. I found a French bloke to drive the van. Claude he was called. He'd never driven before and he knew nothing about bicycles. He couldn't even mend a puncture. Not that it mattered much because I abandoned long before the finish. I had a saddle sore the size of my hand. And the fight had gone out of me. I just didn't care enough to keep going.'

'Do you know what had happened to Henry's brother?' I asked. 'How did he die?'

'Michael – the father of young Michael – was a train driver. For years he drove the London to Exeter night train. Then one night his train severed the head of a woman who'd lain on the line. She just lay down across the tracks. The wheels went clean through her neck. It was dark. Michael didn't see anything. But he knew he'd hit something. He felt it.'

Sarah winced. 'How awful.'

'Ah, it was worse than that,' said Mr Pardoe. 'When they'd picked up the pieces they identified the woman as Michael's wife – Henry's sister in law. She'd suffered from depression for years and she'd tried to kill herself before.'

Sarah and I stared at him, appalled. 'Do you think she knew that Michael would be driving that train?'

'Oh she knew all right. She definitely knew.'

'Poor Michael,' said Sarah softly. 'How awful.'

'He loved her. He was heartbroken,' said Mr Pardoe. 'Couldn't get over it. And two days later he killed himself. He rode his bicycle to the spot where she'd died and he sat down beside the track and carefully cut his wrists with his penknife. Bled to death just a yard away from where she'd died. They found him the next morning. There wasn't a drop of blood left in his body.'

104

'So young Michael lost both his parents,' I said.

'That's right,' nodded Mr Pardoe. 'He was a teenager. Not a kid but still young enough to suffer. He had what they call a nervous breakdown these days. He didn't speak to anyone for months. Not a word.' He paused and fiddled with the tablecloth for a moment. 'I think it would have affected anyone badly,' he said. 'Losing both parents like that.'

'And Henry and Daphne adopted the boy?'

'As far as I know it wasn't ever made official – they didn't bother with any paperwork – but, yes, Henry and Daphne adopted Michael. They treated him like their son.'

'Do you know about Henry taking young Michael's place in the army during the Second World War?'

Mr Pardoe looked at me. 'Oh, you heard about that?'

I nodded.

'Michael got his call-up papers and said he was going to run away. Henry didn't want him to do that. He said that they'd either arrest him and throw him in prison or else he'd be on the run for the rest of his life. Henry said he'd pretend to be Michael and join the army in his place. It wasn't difficult. They looked like one another and there wasn't much age difference. Besides, Henry was very young looking for his age. It was the accident that was responsible for that, I suspect.' He looked at me. 'But you'd know about that.'

I nodded. 'Where did Michael go when Henry went off to war?'

'He came here for a few days. Hid out with us,' said Mr Pardoe. 'Then, when Daphne had sold the garage she and Michael and Michael's fiancée went down to Devon somewhere. They rented a place on the coast.'

'Westward Ho!.'

'That would be it. Westward Ho!. I always thought it was just a book title but it's a real place isn't it?'

'It seems to be.'

'Henry had a real soft spot for the place,' said Mr Pardoe. 'There's a golf course there. Henry used to caddy there when he was young. He loved it. He caddied for J.H.Taylor a few times you know.'

'Who's J.H.Taylor?' asked Sarah.

'He won the British Open Golf Championship a few times. Played his golf at Westward Ho!. He was one of the best in the world. Henry got on well with him.'

'I didn't know about the cycling or the caddying.'

'Ah, he was always shy about things like that,' said Mr Pardoe. 'He lost a thumb in the First World War but he used to tell people it as an industrial accident. I wonder how many people fought in both wars? Can't have been all that many. Not on the front line. There was a strange twist to the war story,' said Mr Pardoe. 'Do you know about the medal?'

I nodded again. 'We found it at a pawn shop in Birmingham.'

'You found the medal?'

'Yes.'

'Henry pawned it?' Mr Pardoe was clearly surprised.

'Yes.'

'He must have been desperate.'

'He was. Is.'

'I'm glad you found it,' said Mr Pardoe. He looked at us both and smiled. 'By and large they didn't hand out medals until after the war,' he went on. 'There wasn't a lot of time for that sort of thing at the time. By the time of the medal ceremony Henry had gone back to being Henry and Michael was back to being Michael. It seemed simpler to stick with that. Even though there were people at the ceremony who'd been rescued by Henry none of them noticed anything when it was Michael who turned up and accepted the medal.'

'And afterwards?'

'It was strange. Getting the medal went to Michael's head. He actually began to believe it was rightly his. There was a bit of publicity in the local paper and he became something of a local hero. Henry told him what had happened so that he'd know what to tell people if they asked. But whereas Henry had always played down what he did Michael gave it a bit of an extra twist. By the time he'd finished telling it you'd have thought he'd lifted up the train single-handedly so that people could be rescued.'

'And Henry got the medal back when Michael died?'

Mr Pardoe nodded. 'Michael – young Michael – died a few years ago. I doubt if he had any other relatives alive. Henry got his medal back when he inherited the rest of Michael's stuff.'

We thanked Mr Pardoe. He went back to his card game. We went back to the car.

★★★

I remembered a conversation I'd had with Henry.

'Having money can be as much of a burden as not having any,' he had said.

When he'd said that I had assumed that he was just telling me a truth that he'd garnered through experience watching other people.

'When you have money you're always worrying about losing it,' he had continued. 'There will always be people eager to take things away from you.'

I hadn't understood why or how he knew this. Now I did.

'Lots of people who are poor are prisoners of their ambitions,' he had said. 'They never live for the now because they are always striving to get somewhere else. But lots of people who are rich are prisoners too. They're prisoners because they're terrified of losing what they've got. And with good reason. There's always someone prepared to steal whatever you have.'

'Live your life accumulating good memories,' he had said. 'No one can take those away from you.'

He'd been right about the money, of course. And now I understood that he was speaking from personal experience. He'd been wealthy; apparently well enough off to satisfy his and Daphne's modest needs. But then he'd lost it all to his dishonest nephew.

But he'd been wrong about the memories. At the time he'd regarded memories as untouchable. But now Daphne was losing those too.

★★★

'People think we're sleeping together,' said Sarah, when we were back in the car.

I looked at her, astonished. 'Which people?'

She shrugged. 'I don't know. Just people.'

'Your boyfriend?'

'Oh no. He doesn't know you exist. And even if he did he wouldn't think you'd dare. Everyone is terrified of him.'

'Including me,' I said. 'I'm in with everyone.'

'You don't even know him.'

'I don't want to.'

'Are we going to look for a hotel now?'

'No. We're going back to Birmingham.'

'Why?'

'Because I can't afford two single rooms in a hotel.'

'I can. Anyway we'd only need one room.'

'No.' I said firmly. 'Thank you. But no.'

'My little problem is pretty well cleared up if that's what you're worrying about.'

'I very much doubt if your little problem is cleared up yet,' I said. 'But that's not why we're going back.'

'Why then?'

'Because I can't afford a hotel. And I'm not letting you pay. I still owe you £60 for the pawnbroker.'

'You're daft. Everyone thinks we're sleeping together so we might as well.'

I didn't say anything. I couldn't think of anything to say. I liked her. I liked her a lot. But I didn't want to sleep with her. My life was confusing enough as it was. She was, I suspected, vastly more experienced than I was. But she also seemed extraordinarily young and innocent. It was a curious mixture. She seemed like a young sister. But I wasn't naive enough and stupid enough to tell her that.

Sarah didn't speak either. We had a long, silent journey.

It wasn't until I was parking the car on the rough ground behind the hotel that she finally spoke. 'Are you queer?'

I laughed. 'No,' I said. 'No, I'm not queer.'

'Have you got someone?'

'No. My last girlfriend left me to marry an estate agent. He had excellent prospects.'

'Are you still in love with her?'

'No.' I said firmly. 'No, I wasn't ever really in love with her.' I paused. 'But I think I'm still a bit bruised. The ending was a bit brutal. I'm supposed to be on holiday in Corfu with her at the moment.'

'I'm sorry.'

'Please don't be.'

'Do you like me?'

'Yes, I do. I like you very much.'

Then she jumped out of the car, pulled her case from the back seat and hurried off towards the hotel. By the time I'd got my bag out of the boot and locked the car she had dragged the darned case half way across the car park. I caught up with her, took the case from her and carried it to the hotel. I then dragged it upstairs for her.

She stood for a moment in the doorway to her room. She held her head to one side, like a bird. 'You're a funny one,' she said.

'I know,' I agreed.

'Can we be friends?'

'Of course.'

'I don't have many friends. Not real friends.'

'No one does. Most people just have lots of acquaintances and contacts.'

She looked down at the floor, clearly thinking of what she wanted to say. 'I always think I have to go to bed with men,' she said softly. I had to strain to hear what she said. 'Otherwise they won't like me.'

'You don't have to sleep with people for them to like you.'

She looked up at me and then smiled and nodded. She kissed me on the cheek, so quickly that I wasn't sure she'd done it. And then the door was shut and she was gone.

# CHAPTER 11

'Somewhere, there has to be a clue,' I said. 'Henry and Daphne would have gone somewhere that was important to them.'

Sarah and I were sitting on the bed in my room at Mrs Potter's small hotel. The George Medal and the bits and pieces I'd recovered from the hospital were spread out between us.

I looked again at the postcards. The messages didn't seem very significant at all. They had all been written during the war and posted to Henry while he was at a training camp on Salisbury Plain. They were all written and signed by Daphne.

'What's on the other side?' asked Sarah.

I turned them over. 'Just pictures,' I said dismissively. 'The usual holiday postcard pictures. A beach. A stretch of headland. A few houses and a slipway. And something that looks like a golf course.'

'They're all the same place,' said Sarah.

'Probably somewhere Daphne was staying,' I said.

'It's that place that Mr Pardoe talked about.'

Suddenly, I felt a complete and utter idiot. Sometimes the obvious is just too obvious. Sometimes I am just unbelievably dense.

'Westward Ho!.' said Sarah. 'It's the only place name I've ever seen that has one of those funny things attached to it.'

'What funny things?'

'Mark things.'

'Exclamation marks?'

'That's it.' She looked embarrassed. 'I was never any good at grammar,' she said. 'But I've always liked books.'

'You're cleverer than I am,' I told her, with a sigh. 'It isn't the writing on the postcards that is the clue. It's the pictures.' I picked up one of the photographs. The photograph of the honeymoon couple. I turned it over and, for the first time, read the name and address of the professional photographer who'd taken the picture. The address was in Bideford. I showed it to her.

'Where's Bideford?' asked Sarah.

'Just a few miles from Westward Ho!.' I hit myself on the side of my head with the palm of my hand. I couldn't believe I'd been so stupid.

'You think that's where they've gone?'

'Of course it is. It's where they were happy. They spent their honeymoon there. They went there on holiday when Michael was a kid. They went there later when they'd adopted Michael. That's where he met Doris. And Daphne went there during the war when Henry was serving in the army.'

'So, what are we waiting for?' said Sarah, jumping to her feet. 'Let's go to Westward Ho!.'

'What about your work?'

'I can't work,' she said firmly. 'I've still got a rash,' she said. 'If necessary I can always get another doctor's note, can't I?'

On her way out of my room she turned. 'Do you really not think I'm stupid?'

'No,' I told her. 'I don't think you're stupid at all.'

She waited and thought for a moment. 'Really brighter than you?'

'Absolutely, definitely.'

She smiled and looked happier than I'd ever remembering seeing her.

'See if you can manage with a smaller suitcase this time,' I suggested.

★★★

After that it was all ridiculously easy.

We drove to Westward Ho!, Sarah and I, and we found Henry and Daphne living in a wooden chalet right by the beach.

The chalet was one of a hundred or so which had been specially built for holiday-makers. They were poorly made and had not survived the Devon storms very well. The one that Henry and Daphne were living in had lost much of the felt from its roof. Two of the window panes had been broken, either by a gale or by vandals, and had been temporarily replaced with pieces of old hardboard.

'Hello!' said Henry. He did not seem surprised to see me. It was a cold, grey, day but he was sitting, in his wheelchair, on a small stretch of cracked concrete outside their chalet. He had a blanket wrapped round his knees. He looked grey and very, very tired.

'This is Sarah,' I said. 'She helped me find you.' I introduced Sarah to Henry.

'Hello Sarah,' said Henry. He wheezed when he spoke. He was having difficulty in breathing. I didn't know whether or not he had any of his tablets with him. 'Would you like some tea? Daphne has just gone in to put the kettle on.'

'I'd love some tea,' said Sarah. Apart from a brief stop for petrol we had driven without a break from Birmingham.

I turned and looked at the view. It was the same beach that appeared on the photographs and the postcards. But it was almost deserted today. There was a man with a black Labrador and a father and two children struggling to control a kite. The Labrador, and the man, both looked old and weary; they each seemed to be walking because the other wanted to. Neither quite understanding that the other would rather be indoors, in front of a roaring fire.

'It's a lovely view,' I said.

'We've always liked it,' said Henry. It took him a great effort to speak.

Just then Daphne came out of the chalet. She was carrying a tray which contained a teapot and two cups. There were no saucers, no milk and no sugar. I took the tray from her and laid it gently on the grass at one side of Henry's chair.

'Would you bring another couple of cups, dear,' said Henry. 'We've got visitors.'

'This is Mrs Mulligan, Daphne,' I said to Sarah. And then I introduced Sarah to Daphne.

Daphne smiled at the two of us and disappeared indoors. A moment later she returned with two cups. These, like the others, were cracked and chipped.

'Shall I pour?' suggested Sarah. She picked up the teapot and poured what should have been tea into the four cups. But it wasn't tea. It was water. There was no steam. The water was cold. Sarah looked at me. I said nothing but reached down and took one of the cups. I gave it to Henry. I took another cup myself. Sarah handed the third cup to Daphne and kept the fourth for herself.

'Thank you, Daphne,' I said.

Daphne smiled and looked pleased with herself. 'They say I've gone loopy,' she said. 'But they're quite wrong.'

'Of course they are,' I said.

We sipped at our cups of cold water. I looked at Henry. There were tears rolling down his cheeks.

'The bad weather is coming in,' I said.

'It is,' agreed Henry. 'There's a hard winter ahead.'

I looked up at the roof of the chalet. A piece of loose felt was flapping in the growing wind.

I knew for certain why he'd come. And I knew what was going to happen.

'I missed you,' I told him.

'I missed you too,' said Henry. He reached up and took Daphne's hand. 'We both did,' he said. He looked at her and smiled. She smiled back at him. There was so much love in their eyes that although it should have hurt to see them that way it did not. I wanted to cry but forced myself not to.

For a while none of us spoke. We just sipped our cold water and stared at the view. The wind got slowly worse.

'Maybe you should go in,' I said to Henry.

'I think you're right,' he said. 'Would you give me a push. Daphne has a bit of a job getting me in through the front doorway. It's a bit narrow.'

I pushed his chair into the chalet. Sarah collected up the cups and put them on the tray. Then she picked up the tray and followed us into the chalet. Daphne followed her.

Inside it was dark and cold.

'There isn't any heating,' said Henry. 'They don't usually let the chalets at this time of the year. But they know me and let us have this one for a few days. We won't be here much longer. We just wanted a little time together in our favourite place.'

I looked at him and could no longer keep the tears from flowing down my cheeks. I heard the door close behind me. I looked around. Sarah had gone. Daphne had sat down in an easy chair. She was just sitting and staring and smiling.

'Sarah seems like a nice girl.'

'She is.'

'Special?'

'A friend,' I said. 'But a special friend.'

Henry looked around. 'This has always been our special place,' he said. He looked at me and smiled. 'I knew you would find us,' he said. He lowered his voice. 'It's all we were waiting for. Just wanted to say goodbye.' He coughed for a few moments. 'We had to take our opportunity to get away from the hospital,' he said.

I nodded. I couldn't speak. I looked around. On the table in the middle of the room there were several bottles of pills. They were drugs that Henry had clearly been saving up. I spotted the bottle of nitrazepam which Sister Tomkins had been looking for. He saw me looking. 'Do you think I'll have enough?' he asked. There was a pause. 'To last me,' he added.

I walked across to the table and looked at the pill bottles. I nodded. 'Plenty,' I said.

'Good,' said Henry. 'I wouldn't want to be short.'

'No,' I said. 'That wouldn't do at all.'

'You'd better go,' said Henry. 'We just waited for you.'

'Why didn't you tell me what you were doing?' I asked him. My voice was faint and I hardly recognised it.

'Couldn't do that,' said Henry. 'You'd have been duty bound to stop us.'

I shook my head.

'No,' he said softly. 'I know you wouldn't.' He held out a hand to me. I took it and gripped it tightly. 'That's why I didn't say anything,' he said. 'Didn't want to put you in that position.'

We stayed like that for a moment. Holding hands and looking at one another.

'I love you,' he said quietly.

'I love you too,' I told him. I wiped the tears away from my cheeks. I didn't think it was possible to cry so much for so long.

'Stay loyal to yourself and your dreams,' he said. 'Don't let the bastards grind you down.'

'No,' I promised him.

''Cus the buggers will try.'

'I know they will.'

'He has to go now,' said Henry suddenly. He had turned his head and was talking to Daphne.

'Oh, must you?' said Daphne. 'So soon? Still it was nice of you to come and see us.'

I put my hand into my pocket and took out a small, red box. I put the box into Henry's hand. He looked down at it. He didn't open it. He knew what it was. He looked up at me.

'Yours, I think,' I said.

He looked at me, tired almost beyond capability, and nodded. 'Thank you,' he said. I could hardly hear him.

'My pleasure,' I said.

I bent and kissed him on the forehead. Then I kissed Daphne. Then I left.

Outside the storm had started. The wind was howling. It was raining hard. Sarah was standing beside the sea wall. Her hair was soaked and so was her face. But I could still see the tears pouring down her cheeks.

'Don't say anything,' she said. 'Not a bloody word. Not one bloody word.'

I didn't.

We got into the car and drove back to Birmingham. We stopped for petrol once. But we didn't speak. There wasn't anything to say.

# CHAPTER 12

'S it down,' said Sarah.

I sat down on my bed.

'I know we're good friends but it would never amount to anything.'

I looked at her, puzzled.

'There's no spark between us,' she said. 'No sexual electricity.'

'No,' I agreed.

'And you're too old for me.'

'Yes,' I said. I was no more than two years older than her. And, I suspected, considerably younger than her boyfriend.

'I'm going to Beirut,' said Sarah.

I stared at her in astonishment. 'Why on earth are you going to Beirut?'

'I've got a fantastic job,' she said. 'Dancing in a club. The chap who hired me said they don't mind girls looking like boys so my small breasts won't be held against me. He showed me pictures of the club. It looks like a palace.'

'What about your boyfriend?' I asked her.

'Oh I've finished with him,' she said, waving a hand. 'He's going out with Jacaranda.'

'Jacaranda?'

'Her real name is Lizzie. She's a hostess at the club.'

'Oh.'

'So I'm off to Beirut! I can get my Equity card.'

'But Sarah,' I said. 'How do you know what they'll expect you to do when you get there?'

'Oh you mean they might expect me to have sex with the customers?'

I went red. 'Exactly,' I said.

'White slavery and all that.'

'Don't laugh.'

She stood on tip toes and kissed me on the cheek. 'There's no problem. The people organising this have got offices in London. They've got embossed notepaper and everything. But you're sweet to care,' she said. 'If I get into trouble I'll phone you and you can ride over there on your white horse and rescue me.'

'OK.' I said.

'We can still be friends, can't we?'

'Definitely.'

'Like brother and sister?'

'Like brother and sister.'

★★★

I went back to the hospital to tell Sister Tomkins what had happened. On my way to the ward I met one of the doctors I'd worked with, a medical registrar.

'Didn't you go off hunting for that bloke who disappeared?' asked the registrar. 'Can't remember his name now. He had lung cancer. Had a loopy wife.'

'Henry Mulligan.'

'Was it? Did you ever find him?'

I nodded.

'Where was he?'

'Westward Ho!.'

'Is that a real place? I thought it was a book.'

'It's in North Devon. Near Bideford.'

'Well, there you go,' said the registrar with a laugh. 'I learn something utterly irrelevant ever day. How was he?'

'He was fine,' I said. Henry had been fine when I'd found him.

'Can't imagine why you wasted your time hunting for him,' said the registrar. 'Just an ordinary old bloke.'

'Oh, not so ordinary,' I said. 'No one is, really, you know.'

'No one is what?'

'Ordinary.'

The registrar looked at me, and raised an eyebrow.

'It's like Chaucer,' I said. 'Everyone has a story. Every life has a tale.'

'You're young,' he said, with a knowing smirk. 'You'll learn.' He hurried off, his unbuttoned white coat billowing out behind him.

I watched him disappear down the corridor and felt sorry for him and for his patients.

★★★

'So what are you going to do now?'

I thought for a moment. 'I don't know.'

'Are you going to get another hospital job?'

I shook my head. 'Hospital work isn't for me.' I remembered something Henry had once said to me. 'In hospital they don't do things for you; they do things to you.' I looked down the ward at the patients lying in their beds. I looked at the man now lying in the bed Henry had lain in for so many months. I would miss Henry. But he would be with me always. He was right about hospitals. I couldn't change the way the system worked. But I could change the way I worked.

I felt the sister's hand on my arm. I turned towards her. 'You're day dreaming.'

I nodded.

'I said, will you go into general practice then?'

'I think I'll give it a try,' I told her. 'One of the GPs in town – a Dr Taylor – has rung offering me a couple of weeks' work looking after his practice while he's on holiday. But in the end I wouldn't mind getting a job as a country GP. An old fashioned family doctor.' I smiled. 'I fancy myself in a three piece tweed suit, a paunch, a fob watch and a big moustached stained by tobacco smoke.'

'You don't smoke!' she laughed.

'I'll dye the moustache,' I said.

# Epilogue

I had arranged for copies of the local paper to be sent to me at Mrs Potter's. I didn't think that Henry and Daphne would make the nationals and they didn't. But they made the local paper. They were on page 14 under the headline 'Couple Found Dead In Chalet'. They were sandwiched between a report of a stolen bicycle and an advertorial promoting conservatory furniture. A policeman was quoted as saying there was no suspicious circumstances and that the dead couple were both elderly and had been ill for some time.

Two days after I received the local newspaper I received a registered packet. The packet had been addressed to me at the hospital and sent on to Mrs Potter's hotel. When I opened it a small red box fell out of the padded envelope. There was a short note with it. The note was in Henry's handwriting.

'Daphne and I want you to have this,' it said. 'Dave, who runs the site, will post it for us. It's the only thing we have of value. Please do whatever you like with it. If you sell it you should be able to get a decent price if you take it to one of the London specialists. It'll be worth the train fare. We both consider you a friend first and a doctor second and although that may sound like a cackhanded compliment it isn't meant to be. Thank you for everything you did for us. Always your friends.' Both of them had signed it though Daphne's signature was rather wobbly.

I had no intention of selling the medal but the day after that I was called by Mrs Potter.

'There's a reverse charge call coming from Beirut,' she called up the stairs. 'Will you take it?'

'It'll be Sarah,' I told Mrs Potter. 'Of course I'll take it.' I raced down the stairs. 'I'll pay for the call,' I promised Mrs Potter. 'You'll do no such thing,' said Mrs Potter, who had a soft spot for Sarah. I picked up the receiver and told the operator I'd take the call.

'You were right about the white slavery,' Sarah said when she was eventually put through. She was trying to sound brave but I could tell she had been crying. 'I've been told that if I don't agree to sleep with the customers they'll just throw me out into the street. They made me hand over the return half of my ticket when I got here and I haven't got enough money for a flight back to Britain.'

'I'll get you some money,' I told her immediately. 'Where do I send it?'

'I saw some chap at the British Embassy. If you send £60 they'll get me a ticket and then I can fly home. But they won't do anything until they've had the money wired through. They say a bank can do it.'

'Where are you now?'

'In a phone box in a hotel,' she said.

'Is it a decent hotel?'

'As decent as anything.'

'Stay there,' I told her. 'Have a cup of tea or something and just wait there. Don't speak to anyone. Don't even look at anyone. Where do they want the money sent?'

She told me.

I took Henry's medal to the pawnshop and persuaded them to lend me £75. I then sent the £75 to the British Embassy. Sarah flew home that evening.

A month later I had saved enough to redeem the medal. I've never pawned it again. I've still got it.

Two weeks after she arrived back in Birmingham Sarah met a car dealer who paid for her to have breast enlargement surgery. She stayed with him for six months and left him when he had an affair with a stripper with a 48-inch bust. She said she wasn't going to go that far to keep a man. But she had more surgery anyway, and then got a job as a showgirl dancing on a cruise ship. After a year of cruising the world and entertaining tourists she married a 63-year-old American oil industry executive and moved to Florida. When he died she married a 67-year-old former banker.

She is now unmarried but a millionairess living in luxury with three Pekinese dogs and a faithful Filipino manservant. I still get a card and a long letter from her every Christmas.

Me?

Well, I'm just me.

Sarah knows I'm writing this and she says she's looking forward to receiving a copy. I promised to send her one with her card next Christmas.

---

For a catalogue of Vernon Coleman's books
please write to:

Publishing House
Trinity Place
Barnstaple
Devon EX32 9HG
England

| | |
|---|---|
| Telephone | 01271 328892 |
| Fax | 01271 328768 |

Outside the UK:
| | |
|---|---|
| Telephone | +44 1271 328892 |
| Fax | +44 1271 328768 |

Or visit our website:

www.vernoncoleman.com

Also by Vernon Coleman

# Mrs Caldicot's Cabbage War

Thelma Caldicot was married to her husband for thirty dull and boring years. The marriage could not have been described as fulfilling in any way, shape of form, but she stuck it out in her usual uncomplaining and subservient way. Then, one afternoon two police officers knocked on her door to bring her some news that was to radically change her life.

*Mrs Caldicot's Cabbage War* is the poignant, warm and often funny story of an ordinary woman who, after being pushed around by other people for most of her life, finally decides to stand up for herself.

Some reviews of *Mrs Caldicot's Cabbage War*

'It's poignant, funny and 'socially relevant'.' DAILY TELEGRAPH

'...destined to be regarded as a typically understated British classic.' EXPRESS & ECHO

'An endearing fairytale quality.' DAILY EXPRESS

'Multi-million selling author Vernon Coleman is behind a big new film comedy. The story, in its paperback novel form, has been lauded as a comedy with an important social message.' HUDDERSFIELD DAILY EXAMINER

'...a little British comedy with a big heart.' FINANCIAL TIMES

'Funny and thought provoking novel. The film has already been hailed a winner at the Chichester and Cannes film festivals, and is showing in many parts of the UK, as well as being on a six month tenure in the picture houses of New Zealand where it has broken box office records. Is there some 'oldie' cult there that we don't know about? Or have they just got good taste?' WESTERN MORNING NEWS

'Vernon Coleman has an impressive list of novels to his credit and this one, first published in 1993, has provided the basis for a newly released film with the same title, starring Pauline Collins as Mrs Caldicot. Humorous, and often touching, this is an entertaining tale with a delightful comeuppance ending.' LEICESTER MERCURY

## Also by Vernon Coleman

'I swung from laughter to tears and back to laughter.'
HAMPSTEAD AND HIGHGATE EXPRESS

'This is the first Vernon Coleman book to get the movie treatment.
It is the latest step in the remarkable career of a man who has brought
unconventional medical wisdom to millions of readers.'
EXPRESS AND STAR

'...a good fun read as well as pinpointing an important social message
for our time. Vernon Coleman is a multi-million selling author, a
former family doctor and television presenter whose 90 books have
been translated into 22 languages and sold all over the world....(Mrs
Caldicot's) cabbage war story is told with laughter, a few tears and a
strong eye on special conditions which need fighting.'
JIM HOWIE, THE CHESTER CHRONICLE

'Mrs Caldicot's Cabbage War...made me laugh out loud. Dr Coleman's
lightness of touch and direct prose are all that one could wish for.'
MAXWELL CRAVEN, DERBY EVENING TELEGRAPH

'...an easy style underpinning a firm social structure...Vernon Coleman's
observations cannot fail to hit home.' NORTH DEVON JOURNAL

'Vernon Coleman really captures the personality of Mrs Caldicot...
You'll be hooked and won't be able to put it down. Vernon Coleman
has written 90 books which have been successful across the globe and
this book can only add to those sales. It is heart warming and funny all at
once.' NEWTON ABBOT & MID DEVON ADVERTISER

'Witty, poignant and beautifully written. A tearful journey into
pensionable age with a glimmer of hope in the laughter.'
WESTERN MAIL

'Humour, pathos and sympathy.' EVENING STANDARD

Paperback £3.99
Published by Great Fiction
Order from Publishing House • Trinity Place • Barnstaple •
Devon EX32 9HG • England
Telephone 01271 328892 • Fax 01271 328768
www.vernoncoleman.com

Also by Vernon Coleman

# Mrs Caldicot's Knickerbocker Glory

Mrs Thelma Caldicot runs a rest home for a bunch of lively old people who enjoy playing volleyball with cushions and cricket with rolled-up socks. But, inevitably, things don't always go quite to plan. The cook turns out to have a fondness for sherry and one of the new residents, a former gardener, decides to dig up the lawn so that he can start growing vegetables.

Just to complicate things further, two employees from the local council make a real effort to close down Mrs Caldicot's rest home. They are aided and abetted by the son of one of the residents who has spotted a way to make a profit if Mrs Caldicot loses her licence.

But there are plenty of bright spots. Mrs Caldicot's romance with newspaper editor Mr Jenkins blooms very nicely – albeit sometimes frustratingly slowly for the two protagonists, neither of whom realise that their feelings are reciprocated. A resident turns out, unexpectedly, to have an apparently endless source of wealth. And a jumble sale and fete is, to the surprise of almost everyone, attended by a clutch of real life movie stars.

*Mrs Caldicot's Knickerbocker Glory* is an uplifting story of how a group of old people, who are overlooked, patronised and under-estimated, overcome adversity, fate, malignant opportunism, greed, envy and spite with integrity, hope and a deep-rooted affection for one another.

"I would like to tell you about what happened when I began reading your wonderful book *Mrs Caldicot's Knickerbocker Glory*. On the first occasion I picked up your book I laughed out loud and felt quite uplifted. I hope to order some books for Christmas presents." MISS O.J., HAMPSHIRE

Hardback £12.99
Published by Chilton Designs
Order from Publishing House • Trinity Place • Barnstaple •
Devon EX32 9HG • England
Telephone 01271 328892 • Fax 01271 328768
www.vernoncoleman.com

Also by Vernon Coleman

# Paris in My Springtime

"A little while ago, while sorting through some boxes I found in the attic, I came across a diary I had kept during a stay in Paris in the last part of 1963 and the first months of 1964. In September of 1963 I had started medical school. But I'd been taken ill and had to temporarily abandon my studies. With the best part of a year to kill I was given two choices: I could either stay at home and get a temporary job driving a fish delivery van or I could go to Paris. After a great deal of thought (which, on reflection, must have taken very nearly a second) I chose to go to Paris. And this is the story of what happened to me that year. Or is it?"

*Vernon Coleman*

"Your books – both fiction and non fiction – are an absolute tonic." MR R.W., SUSSEX

"Just want to thank you for all your wonderful books. Will be buying more soon." M.A., SURREY

"Having read three of your marvellous books so far – I have several more recently purchased to read with great anticipation. I felt I had to tell you how much I enjoyed them." MISS S.H., EXETER

Hardback £12.99
Published by Chilton Designs
Order from Publishing House • Trinity Place • Barnstaple •
Devon EX32 9HG • England
Telephone 01271 328892 • Fax 01271 328768
www.vernoncoleman.com

Also by Vernon Coleman

# It's Never Too Late

Tony Davison is bored, tired and fed up with life. He has lost his job and his wife, and doesn't have much of a future. In despair, he sells his house and most of his belongings and sets off to Paris for a weekend holiday. But what started off as a quick holiday break soon turns into a once-in-a-lifetime experience.

*It's Never Too Late* tells the uplifting story of Tony's search for a new life and happiness in a new country. Full of the gentle humour and anecdotes which are so much the hallmark of Vernon Coleman's novels.

"Imagine that you feel like settling down in a comfortable armchair with an entertaining book – one that will keep your attention and combat the desire to nod off ... If this description fits you then you could do much worse than spoil yourself with this book. The author's style is both easy to read and makes you want to keep turning the pages – in fact I had to force myself to stop reading and put the book down. I am sure you will enjoy the book, which apart from anything else brings to life the atmosphere of Paris – so why not give it to a loved one or friend ... and promptly borrow it to read yourself!? Whatever you may decide, we have chosen this as our Book of the Month."
LIVING FRANCE

"*It's Never Too Late* is a light-hearted reversal of the ageing process." FRANCE MAGAZINE

Hardback £12.99
Published by Chilton Designs
Order from Publishing House • Trinity Place • Barnstaple •
Devon EX32 9HG • England
Telephone 01271 328892 • Fax 01271 328768
www.vernoncoleman.com

Also by Vernon Coleman

# Second Innings

The characters leap from the page as they draw you in to this tale of a young man (Biffo Brimstone) who overcomes the adversity of modern day living by, quite simply, running away! He leaves an unrewarding job, a shrewish and demanding wife and a couple of surly children and takes the next train out of the miserable suburban estate which has been his home for the past few years of his mundane life.

The train takes him to a part of the country he has never before visited, and the subsequent bus journey deposits him in the village of Fondling-under-Water. It is there that his new life begins.

"A piece of good old-fashioned escapism, an easy-to-follow plot; just right to relax with after a busy day ... you would be happy to lend it to your granny or anyone else's granny come to that. This author has the ability to create a distinctive 'mind's eye' picture of every character. The story would 'translate' into an excellent radio play."
THE JOURNAL OF THE CRICKET SOCIETY

"Settling down with Vernon Coleman's latest novel is one of the best restorative treatments I know for relieving the stresses and strains of modern living. Right from page one you can feel yourself unwind as you enjoy the antics of the wonderful array of characters and their exploits. Terrific reading for anyone."
LINCOLNSHIRE ECHO

Hardback £12.99
Published by Chilton Designs
Order from Publishing House • Trinity Place • Barnstaple •
Devon EX32 9HG • England
Telephone 01271 328892 • Fax 01271 328768
www.vernoncoleman.com